Meet the officers of the
Pacific Northwest K-9 Unit series
and their brave K-9 partners

Officers: Parker Walsh and Veronica Eastwood

K-9 Partners: Rosie and Summer the German shepherds

Assignment: Rescue Veronica's kidnapped sister

Officers: Dylan Jeong and Brandie Weller

K-9 Partners: Ridge the Saint Bernard and Chief the bloodhound

Assignment: Stop a bomber out for revenge—and his target is Dylan

Katy Lee writes suspenseful romances that thrill and inspire. She believes every story should stir and satisfy the reader—from the edge of their seat. A native New Englander, Katy loves to knit warm woolly things. She enjoys traveling the side roads and exploring the locals' hideaways. A homeschooling mom of three competitive swimmers, Katy often writes from the stands while cheering them on. Visit Katy at katyleebooks.com.

Sharee Stover is a Colorado native transplanted to Nebraska, where she lives with her husband, three children and two dogs. Her mother instilled in her a love of books before Sharee could read, along with the promise "if you can read, you can do anything." When she's not writing, she enjoys time with her family, long walks with her obnoxiously lovable German shepherd and crocheting. Find her at shareestover.com or on Twitter, @shareestover.

K-9
NATIONAL PARK
DEFENDERS

KATY LEE
SHAREE STOVER

LOVE INSPIRED SUSPENSE
INSPIRATIONAL ROMANCE

Special thanks and acknowledgment are given to Katy Lee and Sharee Stover for their contributions to the Pacific Northwest K-9 Unit miniseries.

LOVE INSPIRED® SUSPENSE
INSPIRATIONAL ROMANCE

Recycling programs
for this product may
not exist in your area.

ISBN-13: 978-1-335-51017-4

K-9 National Park Defenders

Copyright © 2023 by Harlequin Enterprises ULC

Yuletide Ransom
Copyright © 2023 by Harlequin Enterprises ULC

Holiday Rescue Countdown
Copyright © 2023 by Harlequin Enterprises ULC

Love Inspired
22 Adelaide St. West, 41st Floor
Toronto, Ontario M5H 4E3, Canada
www.LoveInspired.com

Printed in U.S.A.

CONTENTS

CONTENTS

YULETIDE RANSOM

Katy Lee

To Jesus, the God of second chances.

Acknowledgments

I want to thank the team of highly talented authors who took part in the creation of the Pacific Northwest K-9 Unit series. I have learned so much from these accomplished writers and consider myself blessed to come alongside them and have my words included in this series.

I also want to thank my editor, Emily Rodmell, for being such an integral part of my career. I have learned so much from Emily through the years. Her wisdom and ability to take my words and make my stories the best that they can be will always be appreciated.

Study to shew thyself approved unto God,
a workman that needeth not to be ashamed,
rightly dividing the word of truth.
—2 Timothy 2:15

ONE

"Jasmin?" Veronica Eastwood called out to her sister through the cabin wall. "Are you all right in there? I heard a noise." Veronica rolled her eyes at how childish she sounded. Jasmin may be ten years older than her, but Veronica was a law-enforcement officer and shouldn't be afraid of strange sounds in the night. She threw back the covers and put her feet in her slippers. Her robe was draped over the bedpost, and she donned it. As she tied it off, the smell of smoke drifted through the room. Had the fireplace been left lit? Veronica remembered putting it out but approached the door to check. She reached for the knob and let out a scream of pain.

Her hand had been burned at instant contact. But how? she wondered as she rubbed at the pain on her palm. It took a moment to register the fact that there must be a fire on the other side. With the knob that hot, she didn't dare open the door.

"Jasmin?" Veronica yelled and banged on the wood, trying to wake up her sister. She went to the wall that separated their rooms in the ski cabin they had rented for the weekend. They were set to hit the slopes in the morning and had gone to their beds an hour ago. A girls' weekend getaway before the Christmas holiday rush.

How could a fire have started? They had been so careful to extinguish the flames that had burned in the fireplace earlier. This didn't make sense.

A glance to the floor showed the smoky mist seeping under the crack. She banged harder on the wall, but if her sister heard her, she wasn't answering.

Had Jasmin already succumbed to smoke inhalation? Her room was closer to the fireplace, so it was possible. Veronica couldn't wait another second. She needed to get to her sister.

Rushing to the only window in the room,

she pushed with all her might to lift it. But the cabin was old, and the window was stuck. With her heart rapidly beating, she stepped back to survey the scene. She only had one choice.

Veronica reached down and grabbed a heavy ski boot by the dresser. The boots had been lined up with a pair of skis to be ready for the morning. With her face turned away, she reared back, then flung the boot through the glass. Flying shards splintered through the room, but most of the windowsill remained. She lifted the other ski boot and used it to knock out the rest of the glass. Turning back, she saw the room was filling up with a cloud of smoke.

"Jasmin!" Veronica called out again as she saw her cell phone on the nightstand. Veronica grabbed it and put it in her robe pocket. She lifted one leg to climb over the window ledge. The drop outside was about five feet into the newly fallen snow that had begun a few hours ago. When she landed, she sunk deep, but quickly trudged to Jasmin's window. They had been so excited when they looked out the cabin window earlier that night to see the snow falling, promising great skiing the next day. A moment later, flames burst through the glass of Jasmin's window, and Veronica turned her body against the explosive sound and heat.

Jasmin was in those flames!

Was she even still alive?

Veronica reached into her pocket and grabbed her phone. She called 911, and a dispatcher told help was on the way, but to get away from the cabin.

"But my sister's in there!" Veronica's voice shook as the freezing snow numbed her feet in her wet slippers. She would be of no help to Jasmin with frostbite. After pocketing her phone, she retrieved her ski boots and headed to the front of the cabin.

As she rounded the building, footprints in the snow stopped her in her tracks. A trail led up to the house. Or away from the house.

Were these Jasmin's boot prints?

Veronica couldn't consider the idea of her sister leaving her in the cabin to perish. And Veronica wouldn't do that to Jasmin either. They had to be someone else's tracks. Someone had to have come here. Perhaps even set the fire.

As Veronica came around the building, she could see the fire was mostly at the back, where the bedrooms were. It was as though it had started in Jasmin's room.

No, Jasmin did not start this fire.

As Veronica rejected her instant speculation about her sister, sirens blared through the North Cascades mountain range. She opened the front door to a cloud of black smoke and coughed. Taking the lapel of her robe, she covered her nose and mouth and stepped inside.

"Jasmin!" she shouted as loud as she could. "Wake up!"

The sirens grew louder as Veronica moved closer to the flames. At some point, she would need to retreat. A wall of fire blocked her from rescuing her sister. No matter what she tried, she couldn't get around it.

"Miss! You need to come out of the house!" a woman firefighter said as she grabbed hold of Veronica's shoulders and pulled her from the cabin.

"My sister's in there!"

"What's her name?"

"Jasmin. She's ten years older than me, and I've always looked up to her," Veronica said in a daze. She wasn't sure why she'd given that information. It just came out. Perhaps, she already knew her sister was gone forever, and that what Veronica had hoped this weekend would do to strengthen their relationship was now for naught.

"Which room?"

"First door on the right." Tears filled her eyes, and she swiped at her cheeks, her hand coming away with wet soot.

"Is there anyone else in the house?" the woman called back.

Veronica shook her head, just staring at the fire as more tears spilled from her eyes. There was no way Jasmin was still alive in those flames. Her sister was gone.

Just when we were starting to build an adult relationship. A friendship even.

"Stay outside," the firefighter ordered her, and then ran forward.

Another fireman draped a blanket over Veronica and led her to the ambulance. Firefighters went to work to extinguish the flames as everything moved in what seemed like slow motion to Veronica.

Then the woman firefighter Veronica had spoken to was standing before her, covered in black soot.

Veronica jumped to her feet. "My sister?"

"Miss? There's nobody in there." Anger covered her face. "Are you positive your sister was in that room?"

"Yes. This doesn't make any sense. We both went to bed over an hour ago." Veronica backtracked the night's festivities. "We cooked dinner and played a card game by the fire. We made sure the fire was out before we went to sleep."

"The fire didn't start in the fireplace. It started in the hallway. And you are the only one in the house."

"My sister was there. Nobody left."

Suddenly, Veronica remembered the single set of footprints, which were probably now trampled away by the trucks and firefighters. She jumped down from the ambulance, circled to the back and saw that the single set of tracks continued into the darkness.

"Where are you going?" the female firefighter called as Veronica followed the tracks.

"These footprints lead from the house. I noticed them earlier." Veronica sighed in frustration. "I wish I had my K-9."

"You're a cop?" the woman asked.

"Yes, K-9 officer. Out of Olympia. My sister and I came up here for a girls' ski weekend. She works for the Pacific Northwest K-9 unit as well, but as a computer tech."

"What's your relationship like?"

"Fine, I guess. I mean there's an age gap, and we've struggled with that. Why?"

"Because if your sister was really here, then she left you in there to die. She might have even started the fire."

"I don't believe that. We may not have been close growing up, but we were starting to be."

The firefighter cast her flashlight beam

on the tracks and into the darkness. The proof appeared before Veronica.

Jasmin had left her behind.

But had she tried to kill her?

"Is this hers?" The woman held up a single glove, which she'd lifted from the snow.

Veronica took it and recognized it instantly as Jasmin's. "Now I really need my dog." She reached into the robe pocket for her phone again and hit the number for the PNK9 Unit, Olympia headquarters.

With Christmas in three weeks, she could only hope someone was in the office to help.

Then a familiar male voice came on the line and Veronica sighed again. But this time in disappointment, as she wished it had been anyone else to answer her call. *Why did it have to be him?*

"Parker, it's me, Veronica. Is Donovan there?"

Veronica's voice sounded off. Regardless of the problems this year with the tryouts to join the PNK9 Unit—four officers vying for two open slots—Parker Walsh wanted her to know she was still important to him. They'd become good friends until everyone, including Veronica, had thought him guilty of the sabotage she and the two other candidates had suffered during the competition. Even though the truth was out that he was innocent—the real villain turned to be Owen Hannington—the friendship they'd once had seemed a thing of the past. In all honesty, he missed Veronica.

"The boss isn't here. In fact, no one is. It's just me tonight. Everyone's on a case, hoping to close them before Christmas." He glanced at the Christmas tree in the corner of the main office space, only half-decorated because the team had dispersed to Washington State's national parks. "What can I do for you?"

Veronica paused, since it sounded like she was walking. He could hear her hesitancy to share what was bothering her. "I'm up in the North Cascades National Park."

"Oh, right—you and Jasmin headed out there for skiing. Should be a great day tomorrow."

"Not anymore. There's been a fire."

Instant panic made Parker shoot to his feet. "Are you all right? Are you hurt? What happened?" He could hear his heartbeat pumping in his head.

"I'm unhurt, but Jasmin's missing. The firefighters found no sign of her in the cabin. I climbed out from my bedroom window and was able to escape."

Escape?

Parker imagined the terrifying incident Veronica was describing and wanted to be there for her. But she was nearly three hours away. "Are they still looking for her?"

"Yeah, but not inside. There's evidence that she left the cabin."

"Well, that's good, isn't it?" Parker sensed her hesitancy. "That she got out in time?" Even saying the words sounded odd. Where was Jasmin now?

And why did she leave Veronica behind to die in the fire?

"Her footprints seem to wander off into the trees. We found one of her gloves. That's why I'm calling. I need the chief to bring me my K-9 right away."

Parker glanced in the direction of Jasmin's office—. "She's a smart lady. I'm sure there must be a valid reason for her to do this."

"I'm hoping so. They think she caused it and..." Veronica's voice trailed off.

"And left you there?" His voice raised in shock.

"Never mind. Could you just have Donovan call me? I don't want him to know about the fire just yet. Just that Jasmin's missing. I'm hoping he can fly Summer up here to help find her. I just need to focus on finding her right now."

"I can bring your partner," Parker said quickly, wincing at his overeagerness. He just wanted to help. At the beginning of the year, she would have done the same.

"Don't come here." Her response came just as quickly. "I mean, just ask someone else, please."

Parker closed his laptop and lifted it from his desk. There was no one else around. All the desks were empty, and the chief's office was dark. He moved to Jasmin's office and opened the door. The lights were off, but the computer screens lit the room with a soft glow. He circled her desk and saw her desk phone's light blinking, signaling a voice mail waiting.

"I'll try my best," he said, feeling rejected by her as he hit the button on the desk phone. Usually, he'd never listen to someone else's messages, but given what was going on…

A man said, "You've been found out. I'm sorry."

The voice mail was cryptic enough, but Parker jerked at the desolate tone in the man's voice. "Veronica, do you know if your sister was in any kind of trouble?"

"Not that I know of, though she was never one to share her problems. Why?"

He held his tongue. There was no sense worrying Veronica more at the moment. He retraced his steps back to the main room, then grabbed his coat from the rack and made his way to the kennels. He hit the code and entered the room, making his way to Summer and Rosie's cages, and unlocked the German Shepherds. They jumped to attention ready to work with their black ears on alert and eyes shining with excitement.

"Get someplace safe. You'll have your partner in a couple of hours. And, Veronica, I'm sure Jasmin will show up." He swallowed hard, praying that was the truth.

"Thank you… Parker. I'm not trying to be mean. I just think it's best if you send someone else."

"I'll do my best."

Parker hung up and called Dylan Jeong for a chopper ride. He was a K-9 officer, as well, and had been with the unit for four years. But he also transported the team to various cases on his rescue helicopter. It would be faster than driving the three hours to the North Cascades. He'd make the call to Chief Fanelli for backup, but when Dylan was ready to fly, Parker planned to be on board, with or without another handler.

He vested and leashed the dogs, then led them out to the parking area. After crating them in his SUV, he started the engine and pulled onto the road. He hoped Veronica would understand that there was no way a friend could leave another friend in the lurch, even if their friendship was technically over.

TWO

"The fire's out, but we'll monitor it through the night in case something is still smoldering," the firefighter informed Veronica as she stepped inside the cabin. She'd learned the woman's name was Chief Rebecca Stine, and Veronica appreciated her thoroughness. "Have the park police found any sign of your sister outside?"

"Not yet."

"I see they brought you some clothes." Rebecca gestured to the National Park Service uniform Veronica had donned when the police showed up. Though Veronica worked in the park, her PNK9 Unit uniform was different from NPS, but she was glad to be out of the sooty, smoky pajamas. "I'm sorry your clothes were burned."

Veronica shrugged. It was the least of her

concerns. Thankfully, she had put her boots by the fireplace earlier in the evening to dry and they hadn't been destroyed. She had placed them next to Jasmin's.

Only Veronica's remained.

More logical proof that Jasmin had left her behind.

The evidence that Jasmin had something to do with this fire was mounting by the minute. The police outside were already heading in that direction. They considered Jasmin Eastwood an attempted murderer and arsonist. There was no proof, of course, but circumstantial evidence made her a possible suspect. When Veronica rejected their assumption, the looks on their faces suggested pity.

"My sister didn't do this," Veronica said to Rebecca. "And as soon as I have my K-9, I'm going to look for her."

"Are you sure you're not too close to this? The evidence is—"

"A lie. We're only seeing what someone wants us to see. I know my sister."

Did she really know Jasmin? The ten years difference between them always kept them from having a close relationship. When Veronica was a teenager, Jasmin was getting married. When Veronica came home from college, Jasmin was going through a divorce. There was always a disconnect between them, maturity-wise. It wasn't until this past year, when Veronica tried out for the K-9 officer position at the PNK9 Unit that she hoped things would change between her and her sister. Four applicants for two slots. Jasmin was the team's invaluable tech expert, and so many thought Veronica would automatically be given one of the positions. No one knew that Jasmin never offered anything to her little sister. They were practically strangers.

"Was she upset about something?" Rebecca asked. It was the same question that the police had asked repeatedly.

And Veronica could only guess the answer.

"We came out here to get away before the holidays. Jasmin put the trip together at the spur of the moment." The more Veronica relayed the series of events, the more Jasmin's actions looked premeditated. At the time, Veronica had jumped at the opportunity to spend the weekend with her older sister. Now that she was a police officer at the same place Jasmin worked, she believed they could be equals in their adulthood.

"Ms. Eastwood?" One of the young park service policemen was standing in the doorway. "The chief wants me to tell you they're picking up one of your colleagues from headquarters. They choppered in. They're being driven over now."

Finally. She didn't dare share her thoughts about Jasmin with anyone but her unit. They all knew Jasmin and would never believe she could kill someone, never mind her sister. "They're bringing me my German shepherd, Summer. Is it Chief Donovan Fanelli?"

"No, I don't think so."

"Luke Stark or Danica Hayes?"

The man shook his head. "Maybe someone by the name of Dylan?"

"Dylan Jeong. Great. He handles mountain rescues. Anyone else?"

Before the man could answer, the sound

of car doors slamming could be heard. Her dog was here.

Veronica bypassed the officer and stepped out onto the porch. One glance at the tall, dark-haired handler leading Summer to the steps had Veronica folding her arms in front of her.

"Parker, what are you doing here? What part didn't you understand when I asked you to send me someone else?"

He stopped at the bottom step and looked up at her. "None of it, because I'm your friend and I want to help. And you have no reason not to trust me."

Veronica bit her tongue from saying trust had nothing to do with her reason for not wanting him there. Every time she looked at Parker, she was reminded of her inability to judge a person's character accurately. It wasn't him she didn't trust. It was herself. When she should think the worst of someone, she didn't. And when she should have stuck up for her friend, she failed to.

Was she wrong about trusting her sister too? So many times, she'd made the wrong choice. And people had been hurt.

Parker was hurt.

"I don't even know why you would want to help me," Veronica said with a sigh.

He frowned and shook his head. "Because I know what it means to make a mistake, and I know if I can't forgive then I'm not forgiven. I accepted your apology, but I have to ask if you actually meant it."

"Of course, I did."

"Then let's put it behind us and find your sister."

Parker held his breath as he waited for Veronica to make up her mind. Would she accept his help or send him away? He lifted the leash that her K-9 was attached to. Her hand reached out to take control of the animal and their fingers touched. In the bright lights that the firemen had set up around the cabin, Veronica's soft mocha skin was a direct contrast to his pale, rough fingers. His years of playing college football had resulted in a few broken fingers that never healed right.

"Thank you for bringing Summer." She looked around. "I was told Dylan also came.

Where is he? We could really use his exper-
tise in mountain rescue." Her glance toward
the dark mountain ranges lifted her face
into the lights of the emergency vehicles.
He wished he could alleviate her worry and
tell her that Jasmin wasn't out there somewhere. But the possibility was there.

"He had to fly out right away. He was
on his way to pick up his niece. Apparently, her parents are having some marital problems, and Leah needs to stay with
him for a while. I was a detour for him.
But I'm grateful he was able to get me here
quickly."

"So you're all I have." She frowned again.

"Well, when you say it like that, I wonder if I'm in the wrong business." He tried
to smile and make light of her disappointment. "But I hope that means you'll let me
stay to help."

She looked over his head to a group of
local police coming out of the woods with
their flashlights bouncing. "They think Jasmin started the fire. They think my sister
tried to kill me." Veronica leveled her gaze
on him. "What do you think?"

Somehow, Parker knew his answer was a test, and if he answered incorrectly, she would send him on his way.

"I think I haven't seen the evidence to make such a judgment. And even if the evidence points to your sister as the main suspect, I would have to consider her character coming before the evidence. I've been down this road before when I solved that murder case back in my hometown. I learned then that nothing is as it seems. To question everything, even the evidence."

Veronica pressed her lips tight. Her delay in answering worried him more. When she spoke, he expected her to send him away. Instead, she said, "Follow me."

From there, she led him and Summer around the fire trucks and police cars until they were out of earshot. "There were a single set of fresh footprints that led from the cabin. They go straight from the building through these woods. On the other side, they come to an end, because they can't go any farther. Parker, they stop on the edge of a cliff." She looked toward the policemen. "They think Jasmin started the fire and then made her way to the cliff. I just can't believe that. I can't believe she brought me up here to kill me, and then..."

It took all of Parker's power not to wrap an arm around Veronica and pull her in close. But he knew the best thing he could do for her was treat this whole case with unbiased professionalism. And that included the way he treated her.

"You mentioned her glove was found. Where is it now?"

She nodded toward the police. "They collected it."

"Let's go get it and have the dogs do a search. The K-9s won't steer us wrong."

". The park service won't let me be involved. They say I'm too close to the case. I'm the victim, and my sister, also PNK9, is their suspect."

"They can't stop us from investigating. Plus, the dogs can help. This is what they have trained for. You were right in calling for your partner." Parker headed toward the officers, then introduced himself.

Once he felt he'd built a rapport with them, he asked for the glove for the K-9s to sniff and seek. He was glad to see, the glove was sealed in an evidence bag with the least amount of human contact. Retrieving his own K-9, Rosie, from the park service vehicle, he offered the glove to her and Summer.

"Seek," he commanded the two German Shepherds.

Parker stood and expected the dogs to head toward the trees where the footprints had gone. Instead, the dogs took steps toward the road. He glanced Veronica's way and saw her startled expression. She may have said she didn't believe the officer's theory of Jasmin going over the cliff, but her surprise suggested otherwise.

The dogs sniffed their way down the long driveway and came to the dark mountain road. They took a right and walked another hundred yards before stopping and taking a sitting position.

"Her scent ends here," Veronica said, kneeling in the snow and looking for more clues and evidence of her sister's whereabouts. Some of the officers had followed the dogs, as well, and now radioed to their team that another scene needed to be processed. Their theory was falling apart, and there was more to this case. Jasmin didn't go toward the cliff, as they'd thought. She came out to the road. Veronica scanned the road. "What was she doing out here? And whose footprints led to the cliff?" Veronica bit her lower lip. "Parker, this makes it look like someone was waiting for her out here. What if she had a getaway car waiting? Maybe the park police are right about her."

"Stop. Don't go there just yet." Parker thought about that cryptic message on Jasmin's office phone. "There's something you need to know. It may mean nothing, or it could be everything."

Veronica stood, giving him her undivided attention. "What is it?"

"Before I left the office to come here, I listened to her messages just in case there was someone she was meeting out here."

"Was there?"

"I don't know, but there was one message from someone saying 'your identity is blown.' Was she hiding from someone?"

He shrugged. "As I said, it could mean nothing—"

"Or it could mean everything. If Jasmin was coming out here for more than a ski weekend, perhaps whomever she was hiding from followed her out here and took her." Veronica's eyes widened. "Parker, we have to find her before…"

As much as Parker wanted to assure Veronica that they would find her sister, the truth was that if Jasmin had been taken from this spot, her scent ended here, and there was no telling in which direction she'd gone.

"I'll refrain from explaining the chances of finding someone who has been moved to a secondary location. You're a cop. You know the drill. But, Veronica, do I need to remind you that someone tried to kill you tonight and that *someone* is still out there?"

"That someone has my sister, and I won't stop until they are taken down."

"I was afraid you would say that." Parker frowned, thinking Veronica really may be too close to this case. "Fanelli would take you off this case in a heartbeat, you know. You were a victim, too."

"Are you going to tell him?"

"I won't lie. That goes against everything I believe in since the day I gave my life to Jesus." Parker paused and hoped he wouldn't live to regret his decision. "But at this point, all Chief Fanelli knows about is Jasmin missing. He knows nothing about the fire, and you being trapped in it."

"Can I trust you to keep it that way?

"I don't like this."

"Neither do I. I don't like having to keep things from the chief, but I have no choice. He'll pull me if he has to consider Jasmin a suspect. If you can't do this, you're free to go."

Parker never felt so conflicted. On the one hand, he wanted Veronica to trust him again, but on the other, he wanted her to stay alive.

Parker nodded once. "I never caused someone's death before. I hope I'm not about to start."

THREE

With the area around the cabin thoroughly searched, the park police cordoned off the cabin with police tape to keep anyone out... including Veronica.

"They're not going to let me be part of their investigation," Veronica said. The police were heading back to park headquarters and didn't invite her to accompany them. "I feel like I'm up against the clock to get to Jasmin before they do. Except, I want to help her, and they want to cuff her."

Parker shut the rear door to Veronica's car. He had just put the dogs inside. "We could head out to Daniel Guthman's lodge. It's the closest one to this place. We could rent some rooms and use the lodge to set up our own base camp. When Donovan sent me out here to help investigate Stacey Stark's murder and find the missing bloodhound puppies, I interviewed Daniel. I think the place could accommodate us all."

Veronica was relieved both cases had been solved. Stacey Stark and her boyfriend had been killed, and the PNK9's rookie crime-scene investigator, Mara Gilmore, had been the suspect until the team uncovered the real murderer—Stacey's business partner, Eli Ballard. They'd owned lodges near all three national parks, but the Stark Lodges would likely go out of business very soon.

As for the bloodhounds, they were back in training for the PNK9 Unit. Veronica had seen them recently and they were in great shape from their long ordeal of having been stolen by a drug runner, who'd used them to find a missing shipment.

"That's the Cascades Lodge, correct?"

"Yes. Daniel had given us some information about Stacey. She had apparently started rumors about his place having mice. She was trying to ruin the lodge competition. This was before she became a Christian. She was working hard to change when she was killed."

Veronica raised her eyebrows at Parker's comment about competition. "Seems like a few people did their best to get rid of competition this year. I wonder if Owen Hannington took his notes from Stacey Stark's playbook." Owen had been one of their fellow candidates until he was caught and arrested. Although there had been only two open slots on the team, the chief had decided to hire all three of the other candidates—Parker, Veronica and Brandie, who was working a case with other PNK9 officers right now.

"Both their outcomes prove that there is a better way to get ahead—just saying."

As Veronica sought the eastern horizon, she thought about Owen Hannington and his attempts to get rid of two of the hopeful candidates for the K-9 officer slots. She had believed him to be a good person until his true colors had been revealed. Once again, she was reminded of her inability to judge a person's character. She opened her car door, climbed in and said sharply, "Daylight will be here soon, and mice don't bother me. Let's get over to the Cascades Lodge and try to get a few hours of sleep. We need to start our own search first thing."

As soon as Parker climbed into the passenger seat, Veronica headed down the driveway, slowly passing the last place there was any evidence of her sister. Had someone picked her up? Perhaps she was already gone before the fire started and someone came back to light the flame. Someone who wanted the police to think Jasmin started it.

"Take the next right," Parker instructed her. "I know a faster route to get to the lodge. It's off the main road, but we'll come in through the back way, around the lake."

Veronica took the turn. "About that message that you heard on my sister's voice mail."

"What about it?"

"I've been thinking about the fact that perhaps Jasmin had come out here to meet with someone. I had thought it was about a bonding weekend with me, but I can see now that wasn't the case."

Parker looked her way and frowned, the

glow of the dashboard lights partially illuminating his handsome face. She may doubt her ability to be a good judge of character, but she didn't doubt that she knew a handsome man when she saw one. And Parker Walsh fit that bill.

"I think your sister wanted this weekend with you. Even if she did come out here to hide or meet someone else, she wanted you near for a reason. Jasmin always has our best interests at heart. She may think analytically, but that's what makes her the greatest asset in our unit. She has our backs and is always a step ahead of us logically. She knows what needs to be done to keep us safe. She knew what she needed to do to keep you safe."

"You're talking about her like she's still alive."

"I believe she is. She would've had a plan B and even a plan C. That's the way her mind works."

Veronica drove on in silence, considering Parker's accolades in reference to Jasmin. She wanted to believe everything he'd said.

But Jasmin had left her behind.

It was a fact that Veronica could not get past. If her sister was in trouble, why hadn't she confided in her when they were playing cards in front of the fireplace? Why did she say she wanted to turn in early and get a good night's sleep to be refreshed for their ski day the next morning? Why did she put on her boots and walk out the door?

There was only one set of footprints, so how did the fire start, and when?

The car slipped on some ice, and Veronica struggled to right the wheels. "Perhaps coming off the main road wasn't a good idea. These roads haven't been plowed as well as the main roads."

"You're right. I didn't even think of that. We're almost there, though. It's just around the backside of the lake now."

Veronica gripped the steering wheel with both hands and brought her speed down to almost a crawl. There were also no street-lights on the side of the lake. She kept her high beams on to see as far as she could in front of her, and her rearview mirror showed another car off in the distance.

"At least we're not alone out here. Someone else is driving behind us. If we go off the road, they'll find us." She was joking but was still glad to see another car out here.

Parker glanced at the mirror on the side of his car. "That car has been there the whole time. I noticed it when we pulled away from the cabin."

"And you didn't think to mention it?"

Parker shrugged. "We passed plenty of cars. I haven't mentioned any of them. It's quite normal to see cars on the road." He smirked her way.

"But this one came off the main road with us."

"True. I appreciate your deducing skills. Let's see if he follows us into the lodge parking lot. It's the next right."

Keeping an eye on the rearview mirror, Veronica drove the rest of the way around the lake until she saw the sign for Cascades Lodge. She turned in and slowed her vehicle to wait and see if the car would keep driving by. She saw the lights first and then watched the car pull in behind her.

Casting a glance Parker's way, she said, "That's too much of a coincidence."

"I agree." He retrieved his sidearm and readied it. He opened the door and got out quickly, then opened the back door. "Rosie, come." The dog jumped out upon command, and Parker approached the passenger window of the car behind them.

Veronica got out, as well, and retrieved Summer, only she did not have her gun with her on the trip. But the guy behind her didn't need to know that.

As she approached the driver's window, the man behind the wheel had his hands up. "Veronica? It's me, Tyrese. Tyrese Turner. Your sister's ex-husband."

It took Veronica a few seconds to register the man sitting behind the wheel as being her former brother-in-law. She hadn't seen him for three years—since the divorce. It made no sense for him to be here now.

"Why are you following me?"

"I wasn't sure it was you at first. I was looking for Jasmin." He moved his hand to reach inside his coat.

"Hold it right there. Show your hands,"

Parker said, leveling his gun at the man through the passenger window.

Tyrese put his hands back up again. "I just want to get my phone to show you the message I got from her."

Veronica sent Parker a quick look over the hood of the car. At his nod, she said, "Slowly."

Tyrese carefully reached into his coat and removed the phone, showing it to her. "I'm not armed. Here, take it and see for yourself." He passed the phone through the window and Veronica reached for it. "She gave me the address of the cabin and told me to come quickly."

"What does it say?" Parker asked.

Veronica relayed the text message. "'Tyrese, I'm in danger. In case I don't make it, please know I forgive you.'" She looked over the car again. "She gives the address of the cabin and tells him she needs help."

Tyrese continued, "When I got near the cabin, I saw you pulling away—and that the cabin was cordoned off. I quickly went back out to the road and started following you. I thought maybe you were Jasmin. Where is she?"

"I find it hard to believe that Jasmin would contact you. Have you even spoken to each other since the divorce?"

Tyrese shook his head. "Not at all. That's why I thought it was weird. She would've had to have been in dire straits to reach out to me now."

Veronica glanced up at Parker and nodded. "Maybe this was her plan B."

Tyrese huffed. "The way things ended with Jasmin and me, I would have to say I would be her plan Z."

Veronica would have to agree. She scrolled the phone to see if there was any other conversation, but this was the only message.

"I take it I got there too late," Tyrese said. "Is she alive?"

"That's what we're trying to find out. At some point tonight, she disappeared." That was all the information Veronica was going to share with this man from Jasmin's past. Although, the message on his phone definitely came from Jasmin's number.

"As you can see, I texted her back. Her

text came in at ten p.m., and when I didn't hear anything back after my response, I headed out here at midnight. I didn't mean to scare you. I just don't know what to do. I wasn't going to ignore her plea for help, regardless of our history."

Veronica had to admit the man had a viable reason for being out here. She would've done the same thing. She glanced at Parker, then asked, "What do you think?"

"I think this is your call. You know this man. I don't."

Yeah, but I trust your judge of character over my own.

The headlights of another car came down the road, and a glance to her right showed the vehicle slowing down. Just as Veronica thought it would turn into the lodge parking lot, the shadow of a man leaning out the passenger window with a gun registered in her mind.

"Get down!" she shouted. Three gunshots burst out from the gun and the car sped off.

Veronica threw herself to the ground over Summer just as Tyrese's side mirror blew off, right where she had been standing. She could hear Parker running around the car as the blasts of the gun echoed in her ears.

"Veronica! Are you hit?" Parker shouted as he touched her arms and face. The dogs barked loudly around her and wanted to go to work. But the shooter was gone.

"We need to go after him," she said, pushing herself up.

"Were you hit?" Parker asked again.

She shook her head. "I don't think so. I saw the shadow of the gun before he took the shots." She did a mental check of her own extremities as she stood up.

Then she saw Tyrese slumped over the steering wheel.

"He's been hit," she said, opening his car door. "Tyrese! Can you hear me? Parker, get me some light so I can see him fully."

Parker ran around the front of the car and opened the passenger door to put the interior light on. Together they brought Tyrese back against the headrest. His head lolled to the right and he groaned.

Veronica pocketed Tyrese's phone to feel his head for where a bullet may have gone in. She could find nothing until she felt the back of his left shoulder. Her hand came away sticky. But in the dark, she couldn't determine if there was an exit wound.

"We need to get him up into the lodge in case these men come back. The bullet might still be inside of him." She pulled Tyrese's phone out to dial 911. "I'm calling an ambulance."

Parker looked at her and said, "We need to get *you* into the lodge before these men come back. This bullet was meant for you, just as that fire was. In case you're not following, those gunshots were their plan B. And neither have worked." He passed her his gun. "Take it. I have my personal sidearm too. You can expect them to circle back for plan C any time now and need to be able to shoot first."

FOUR

Tyrese moaned as they led him into the lodge. He gripped his arm with his other hand and leaned into Veronica as she finished the call to the dispatcher. The lights to the lodge were low, and the early morning staff were just arriving. A woman from the kitchen stepped out from a swinging door with a white apron tied around her round midriff.

"Can I help you?" she asked as she came closer.

"I'm Officer Walsh and this is Officer Eastwood. This man was shot outside, and we need to help him. Where can we lay him down?"

"Oh, my! What is this world coming to? Right this way." The cook ambled down the hall with dark wood paneling and dim light. She led them to an open great room, where a fire had already been lit in the fireplace. Couches filled the room in different places, and Parker chose the closest one to put Tyrese on.

"I need to remove your coat and shirt to inspect the wound," Parker said.

Tyrese moaned loudly but nodded and let go of his arm to give Parker access to the coat.

The woman said, "I'll be right back with some clean towels and the first-aid box." She disappeared down the hall in the direction they had come.

"I knew coming here was a big mistake," Tyrese said. "I should've just deleted that text."

"Why didn't you?" Veronica asked as she helped remove the shirt next. "As far as I knew, Jasmin never had any reason to speak to you again. I don't know much about your divorce, but I know it wasn't amicable."

Tyrese frowned and sighed. "Maybe that's why I came. I'll admit it. I was a horrible husband to her. When she filed for divorce, I wasn't surprised. I thought this might be a way to make up for the way I treated her. A second chance to help her. Maybe even have some closure for the both of us. That's all."

Veronica cast a glance toward Parker, but he wouldn't tell her how to feel. However, he understood how the man felt.

"There was a time I acted horribly myself," Parker said. "Veronica can attest to my arrogance when I came on the unit. I thought because I had a murder case under my belt, I had something to brag about. I know now I'm only as good as my team. When my team is hurt by my actions, nothing goes right."

Veronica glanced up from inspecting Tyrese's wound. "But you're not that person anymore." To Tyrese, she said, "Parker here had a coming-to-Jesus moment and turned his life around. Have you had something similar, Tyrese?"

He winced when she prodded the back of his shoulder. "Can't say that I have, but I've learned my lesson. I lost a good woman, and for that, I'll never forgive myself."

Parker said, "Forgiving yourself is important, but it starts with accepting God's forgiveness first. It's accepting that not all the people we hurt will forgive us, though. That's what's hard." If Veronica was listening, he couldn't tell. Her full attention was on the wound.

"Believe it or not, I think the bullet just grazed you," she said. "You have no puncture wound at all. Just a slice of your skin taken out. The bullet that hit the side-view mirror is probably the one that grazed you. I'd say you've been given a second chance at life."

The cook returned with the towels and first-aid box. "The ambulance just arrived. I'll bring the paramedics in."

Veronica replied, "He should be fine. But it's up to you, Tyrese if you want to see a doctor to be sure. That's your call."

"It might not hurt, I suppose," he said. The man looked like he might be going into shock just from fear. "Just to be sure. I've never been shot at before."

Veronica opened the kit and swabbed an antiseptic against the wound. She took a large bandage and put it over it. "I'll go give my statement to the police."

"Wait," Parker said, and stopped her. "It's not safe out there for you. Let me talk to them first."

"Parker, I witnessed the whole shooting unfold. I saw the car. I saw the gun. It was too dark to ID the shooter, but I can give a description of the car. You can't do any of those things because you were watching Tyrese. You don't have eyes behind your head. The faster the police can track this car down, the faster I can get my sister back."

Tyrese looked up at Veronica. "You think these guys took Jasmin?" Panic filled his voice, and his brown eyes widened.

Parker shook his head at Veronica to hold off speculating in front of the man.

"We know nothing at this point," she replied, her eyes showing her weariness. She needed some sleep.

"You'll be no good to your sister if you're dead on your feet. Literally." Parker stood. "What kind of car?"

She pressed her lips tight, but replied, "Dark full-size sedan, two-door."

"I think I can handle that." Parker headed to the hallway. "I'll also see about getting us rooms."

He stopped when Veronica called out, "What about him?"

Parker turned his head and had to make a quick assessment of Tyrese Turner. He seemed legit and had been shot tonight. Thankfully, the bullet missed him. "I trust your judgment to decide," he told Veronica.

"How did I know you would say that?" She sent him a scathing look.

Parker smiled and headed to give a statement to the police. "And I meant every word of it."

"All right. Send in the paramedics for him. They can take him."

"You got it."

When he reached the responding officers, he figured out right away that they were already considering this shooting Jasmin's second attempt to kill Veronica. It only proved Veronica's judgment was on point with them, as well. They would be of no help in keeping her alive as long as they were chasing the wrong suspect.

By the time Veronica entered her room at the lodge and found a bed to lay her head on, the sun was coming up. But she needed to get a few hours of sleep at least. Parker was right—she would be no good to her sister if she was exhausted. He also told her the police felt the shooting was Jasmine's second attempt to kill her. Veronica needed to find her sister before they did.

"What's our plan?" she asked Parker as she stepped into the lobby of the Cascades Lodge, barely feeling refreshed but ready to go. He was at table, poring over a map by the towering Christmas tree decked out with white lights. He'd found a red-and-black checkered flannel and looked like he was modeling for a men's outdoor catalog. "Nice shirt."

"Daniel Guthman, the lodge owner, has outfitted us from his gift shop. Down jackets, gloves, boots, ropes and knives."

"Ropes and knives?"

Parker tapped his pointer finger to a place

on the map. "Our first stop is at the bottom of the cliff, where those footprints led to above."

"But if they weren't my sister's, what's the point?"

"It's a start."

"Or it was meant to throw us off."

"The police will check it out. Do you want to beat them to it, or not?" Parker rose to his full height. The tilt of his chin reminded her of his arrogant days. Had he really changed, or was she witnessing his prideful side come out again?

Veronica stepped up to the table to see the map. "This is more than seeking competition. I'll go down there because I seek justice. True justice. And what the police are after is not that. They just want to close this case. I want my sister back."

"And I want you safe." Parker walked around the front of the table, coming face-to-face with her. "Someone has gone to great lengths to kill you, and we need to figure out why. They're coming back."

"Good. Let them. They'll lead me to my

sister. Have you talked to the chief this morning?"

"No, not yet. I'll call him when we have a plan formed. I also didn't want him to know we aren't working with the local police. We may need him to send us a few officers to assist. Tyrese went to the hospital to be checked out, but says he plans to return to help find Jasmin."

"I suppose that could help. It's three weeks before Christmas. Everyone else is strapped with their own cases to close up." Veronica shifted to view the map. "And I can't wait. Every moment that goes by decreases my chances of finding her..." Veronica left out the word *alive.*

"That cliff's not going to be easy to get down. There's a path, but it's treacherous. Are you sure you're up for it?"

"I have an idea." Veronica grabbed her phone from her back pocket. "Jasmin and I were planning to heli-ski. We signed up for drop-offs at the top of the mountain, but perhaps we can arrange for a different location to be dropped off at."

She gestured toward the map and watched

a slow smile spread on Parker's handsome face. Her toes curled at the sight, but she wasn't about to share that information with him. She liked him better without his chest puffed out in pride. She wanted this new Parker to stay, but that meant he could never know how attractive she found him. That was a secret she would take to her grave.

FIVE

"This is where you want to be dropped off?" the helicopter pilot, who was sitting beside Parker, said through the headset. Veronica was with the dogs in the back. The pilot leaned to his right to survey the area. "I'm not sure I can find a level spot close by. You might have to hike in."

"We're prepared for that," Parker said, gesturing to the stocked backpacks at his feet. "Take us down wherever you think it's safe."

The pilot moved farther north before lowering the chopper on a wide area. Behind them, the cliff by the cabin showed at least a hundred-foot drop. Snow-covered rocks and trees abutted the cliffside, suggesting a deadly landing if someone had jumped or been thrown over. Parker kept that thought to himself, but he could tell by Veronica's worried expression that she was wondering the same thing. There may have only been one set of footprints in the snow, but that didn't mean someone hadn't carried Jasmin to the cliff's edge and thrown her down.

The pilot said, "Call me if you need a lift out. Hopefully, you'll keep service." Veronica exited with the two German shepherds, and they all sank a little in the deep snow. He continued, "Careful of where you step. The snow is deceiving. One wrong footing could send you free-falling into nothing below."

Parker said, "We'll be tethered. If one goes down, we'll be able to stop the fall."

"You sound prepared. But I have to ask you—if you're cops, where's your team?"

Parker didn't need this conversation. The guy wouldn't understand the need to go rogue. Parker was even having trouble with it. It wasn't a good direction for his career or his character. "We're with the PNK9 unit in Olympia. One of our own is missing, and we can't wait for the others to arrive. Time is critical."

That much was true, and he did hope Chief Fanelli would arrive soon. It wasn't a total lie.

Parker guided Veronica and the dogs away from the helicopter as it lifted off the ground to head back to its home base. They bent with their arms raised to shield their faces from the flying snow the rotating blades threw, and once the motor grew distant, they straightened and roped up.

Veronica tested the dogs' knots and then secured her own. She scanned the area, then said, "It looks like there's a safe but long route back to the cliff, and a faster but harrowing one. I'm tempted to take the faster route."

"Why did I know you were going to say that?" He gestured for Rosie to take the lead. If the ground under the snow disappeared, he could catch the dog a lot easier. Veronica moved next, followed by Summer.

"At least the sun is shining," Veronica said. "It feels good on my face."

"Stay focused."

Veronica turned her head. "When have

I not been focused? What are you insinu-
ating?"

Parker bit back a laugh and raised his
hands. "Hey, I was just thinking of your
safety through here. That's all."

She pursed her lips. "Are you sure that
wasn't a dig about misplacing my badge
and gun? Because that hadn't been my
fault, and you know it."

Parker remembered back to the sabotage antics Owen Hannington had carried
out on all of them. Veronica and Brandie
had taken the brunt of the attacks, and the
man had made it as if Parker was the cul-
prit. Even though the truth was out now, it
seemed by Veronica's annoyance with him,
he was still paying for them.

"You're a good cop," he said. "I never
doubted that." *Even though you doubted
me.*

Parker reined in the old hurt. He had forgiven her but still wished it had never happened. What would they have become if
the sabotage hadn't separated them? They
had been on their way to becoming great
friends, perhaps even partners. They had

each other's backs, and as Parker walked behind her now, he wondered if Veronica would still have his if the going went rough. Forgiving her was one thing, but that didn't mean he could trust her to be there for him when he needed her most.

It didn't matter, he decided. He would give his life protecting her if he had to. He would have to answer for his choices someday, and the decision to protect her was what he would do, regardless of how she felt about him.

Still, it hurt to think about how she had been so quick to point the finger at him during the sabotage.

Veronica turned back around and kept walking. Even though they were tethered together, Parker felt the distance between them grow. He didn't think she would say another word to him but then she quietly spoke.

"Thank you, Parker. Believe it or not, your confidence in me means a lot."

He smiled at the back of her head. She had on a white knitted hat with a pompom on top that bounced with each of her steps through the snow, and he found it endearing. They didn't have much to choose from in the lodge gift shop, but he figured Veronica would make a potato sack look becoming.

"Hey, Parker?" Veronica stopped short. "I think Rosie is alerting."

Parker glanced around Veronica to see his K-9 straining forward. "She senses something, but I didn't instruct her to seek your sister or anything. Let her take the lead but be careful."

A tenseness settled around them as they focused on their surroundings while Rosie led them to something or someone. Parker withheld his thoughts of the possibility of finding Jasmin at the bottom of the cliff. He knew Veronica was already thinking the same thing. He prepared himself for his next move if that happened. He would need to be there for her, but he doubted she would let him. Whatever Rosie was about to find may create an even wider chasm between them.

The dog strained and pulled as Veronica and Parker sped up to give her the lead.

They plowed through the snow until they reached the rocks abutting the cliffside. Parker strained to see what was out of the ordinary ahead of them. With his gaze set straight ahead, he nearly missed the shift below them. The sight of Veronica sinking pulled his attention from the cliff to her as his arms reached out to grab her before she fell. Only she wasn't falling. She was sinking.

"Veronica!" he shouted as he felt his own feet sink.

She let out a shriek as she also struggled to gain her footing. Her arms lifted high as she lost her balance and dropped below the snow in an instant. Her scream ricocheted off the surrounding cliffs.

Parker felt the instant tug of the rope pull him down with her. With nothing nearby to grab hold of, stopping himself from falling through the snow proved to be nearly impossible. He turned to yank Summer back with him as their weight offset the weight of Veronica and Rosie on the other end of the rope.

A precarious balancing act ensued that could turn deadly with one wrong move.

"What do you see below you?" Parker asked, attempting to remain calm. He bit down as his muscles strained to hold his body still. What if the snow swallowed him too?

"Nothing but darkness. Parker, it looks like a bottomless pit."

Parker felt his body tense. "I was afraid of that. This must be what Rosie was alerting us to. She must have sensed the change in the ground vibrations and knew there was a crevasse beneath us." He took a slow, easy breath and scooted back another foot, glad to see he was able to bring the other two up from the glacial gap, as well.

"I've got Rosie," Veronica said, her voice strained. "I was able to grab her before we dropped too far."

"Thank you for that. She must feel a little better having you hold her."

"I don't know how much longer I can. She's heavy, and I have no footing. I'm just dangling here."

Parker put his gloved hands behind him in

the snow and pulled his body back another foot. If there was no land below him, he wondered when he too would fall through. If he reached a weak point, it wouldn't take much to break through the hard-packed snow. One crack under his weight would be all it took.

"Hold on. I'm going to do this slowly and carefully." He shifted backward again.

He pulled himself back one more foot, then another, until finally, he saw Veronica's pompom surface from below. She turned enough for him to see the fear in her eyes, but the clench of her jaw suggested determination. She would not let go of Rosie if her life depended upon it.

Parker faced a decision he never thought he would have to make.

"Veronica, it's—"

"Stop. Don't even go there. Just focus on pulling us up. You can do this." Her vote of confidence in him seemed foreign after months of her believing the worst in him. But then, what choice did she have in this moment? What choice did *he* have? He had no plans to detach them from his side of the rope. He pushed away the creeping thought as more impossible than following them down the crevasse.

Then the snow below him cracked and he shifted downward on a jolt.

"Parker!" Veronica's brown eyes implored him.

"Shh." He lifted his hands and stilled his body. "Don't move."

For the next few thudding heartbeats, they stared at each other as they waited to see if they would all go in.

Parker felt Summer behind him sniffing the ground.

"She's seeking," Veronica whispered. A faint proud smile twitched on her trembling lips. In any other situation, Parker would have found the moment touching between the handler and her K-9. Instead, he felt anger well up inside him. It was as though Veronica was giving up hope and accepting her demise.

Summer sniffed to his right five feet away and sat. She had found secure land, but if he moved one inch, he would take them all down.

"Good girl," Veronica said, but when she glanced Parker's way, he could tell she knew it didn't matter. It might as well have been a million feet away. As strong as Summer was, if the rest of them caved in, Summer would follow them all down.

"I need to detach myself from you three."

"You can't be serious." Veronica's eyes widened.

"Just hear me out." Parker raised his hand. "Summer will be able to hold you better without my weight. I want you to slowly turn toward her and encourage Rosie to jump up beside her. The two of them will be able to hold tight on your rope so you can pull yourself up."

"But what about you?" Uncertainty threaded her voice.

Did he sense sorrow in her words? They both knew if he fell through, they could all be dead, depending on how far the drop was to solid ground. But did the idea of him not making it sadden her?

"I didn't know you cared." The words slipped out, meaning to be a joke, even if it was a bad one at the moment.

She averted his gaze, glancing past his shoulder. "I didn't either," she said under her breath. Her eyelids dropped closed, then opened as she nodded. "Okay. I'm ready, but can I pray for you first?"

Parker felt his mouth drop and his heart swell. "I would love that. Thank you, Veronica."

"Don't thank me yet. I'm not very good at it."

Parker smiled and wished he could reach out to her. He dared not move a muscle and said, "Don't overthink it. God loves to hear from us. Just speak from your heart. What do you want to tell Him?"

"I want to tell Him that this is so unfair, but that sounds like complaining."

"Well, why do you think it's unfair?"

"Because you don't deserve to die. I mean, sure, you were arrogant when you first came to the unit, but that doesn't mean you should give up your life helping me now?"

"We're cops, Veronica. We vowed to serve and protect and put our lives on the line. And you aren't safe yet. I need to get you to Summer first. So pray for that."

At her nod, she began, "Dear Jesus, I only wanted to find my sister. She's in danger, and now, so are we. I ask You to guide her home." Veronica captured his gaze with softer eyes than he had seen from her since Owen's sabotage. "And make a way for us too. Somehow, make a way."

"Don't give up hope. You're going to get out of here, and you're going to find your sister. God heard you. Are you ready?"

"No, but I don't have a choice, do I?"

"Nope. On the count of three, guide Rosie up to Summer. She'll jump up. Then you pull yourself up quickly and let them anchor you. You have to be fast."

"I will."

Together they counted, and right on cue, Veronica followed the directions perfectly. She turned and hefted Rosie up to secure ground. The K-9 took a strong leap and ran past Summer until the rope stopped her. The momentum gave Veronica an added edge, and she used it to make her own leap, holding on to the rope that attached her to the dogs. Swinging a leg up at the same moment brought her to solid ground.

As much as Parker wanted to help, he dared not move. Pride swelled in his heart. "I knew you could do it."

Veronica was lying on her stomach, facing him. She lifted her gaze as her deep breaths leveled out. "Now, your turn." Just as she shimmied forward, Parker unclipped himself.

"I'm not taking you down with me," he said as the snow below him cracked, and he felt his body drop through.

SIX

Veronica and Parker hadn't gone through all the turmoil of the year to have it end like this. As she watched Parker cave in, she lurched herself forward as far she could and grabbed hold of his coat's collar. His body jerked to a stop as the snow gave way to the deep crevice below.

"No, Veronica!" he yelled, his face panic-stricken. "Back away now. It's not safe."

She clamped her jaw tight as she pulled with all her might to bring him toward her. "Hold on to me," she said, struggling to get the words out. Her arms shook with exertion.

Thankfully, he complied. She didn't have the strength to argue with him. Her only focus was to pull him up quickly while she had snow beneath her. There was no telling how long it would last.

Parker did his best to help her lift his weight, and as soon as he fell to the snow, the cracking sound alerted them to its weakness. Veronica couldn't stop yet. Pushing past the last bit of strength she had left, she pulled Parker toward the dogs.

"Hold!" she commanded them.

The dogs rushed in and latched on to them both, to keep them from sinking. Veronica and Parker lifted up on their elbows and crawled quickly, finally collapsing on their K-9s in relief.

When Veronica could open her eyes again, she found Parker staring at her.

"You saved me," he said. He sounded surprised. But then she hadn't been the warmest person to him lately. Still, that didn't mean she wanted him dead.

"It's part of the job, right, girls?" She cast her gaze at their K-9 partners.

"Right," he replied quietly. "Thank you. To you all." He reached a hand to the dogs' heads for a pat.

Veronica felt uneasy and tested her weakened arms, pushing herself up to sit. "We need to keep moving." She gained her feet. "Tether yourself to us again." She held the rope out to him as he looked up at her with those endearing blues. "And stop looking at me like that."

He stood, cracking a lopsided smile her way. "Like what?"

"Like you want to hug me or something."

"Well, you did just save my life. It would be appropriate."

"It doesn't mean it's going to happen." Veronica moved to step away and head toward the cliff.

That's when she saw something black on the rocks. It was broken but it looked like a phone.

"Parker, could that be Jasmin's phone?" She raced forward, forgetting they were all tied together. She was pulled back until the dogs and Parker picked up their speed to let her take the lead. As soon as she reached the busted phone, she knew it belonged to her sister. "Had she thrown it down from above? Or had the person who took her tossed it over the cliff?"

Veronica reluctantly scanned the area, wondering if she would see Jasmin's dead body down here too. But there was no sign of any disturbance in the snow or rocks. Nothing but the phone.

"I'd say someone tossed it to lead us astray. Or..." Parker said, removing Jasmin's glove from his backpack and placing it under the dogs' noses. "Jasmin left it here for us to track. But let's be certain she's been down here. Seek."

Rosie and Summer went to work sniffing the area, climbing on the rocks and down the other side. Veronica expected them to search in circles, but they continued to move.

"Veronica!" a voice called from above.

She looked up at the top of the cliff and saw Chief Donovan Fanelli had arrived from headquarters. She waved an arm, thankful for unbiased help.

"We're down here." Glancing back at the way they'd come down, she saw the gap that would now prevent them from returning. "The snow gave way, and we're stuck down here."

"I'm glad to see the two of you alive. What have the dogs found?" Donovan asked, pointing to the K-9s, who were still sniffing.

Parker replied, "They're tracking Jasmin. We found her phone down here, but there's a chance she was also down here too if they've picked up her scent."

Veronica followed the dogs and soon saw footprints. "Someone's been here!" she shouted, picking up her steps and pulling Parker behind her.

"Wait," Parker called, but he continued along.

"I can't. They've tracked her. Jasmin was here. She came down that cliff." Veronica didn't want to imagine her sister falling, but how else could she have gotten down? And where was she now?

Veronica looked around to see if there was evidence of an animal dragging a body away. But these tracks were human. If Jasmin was here, she walked out on her own.

But where did she go? And why?

Parker kept up with Veronica and the dogs, but as the sun went down, he knew he would have to stop the search. Whenever he brought it up, she shushed him and pushed forward.

"Look, I want nothing more than to find your sister, but we are not prepared to be out in the elements all night long. We have to head back."

"We're close. I can feel it."

"We're not even sure we're following the right tracks. We've lost them three times and picked up another set. These could be anybody's."

She kept walking in front of him as though she didn't hear him.

"Thirty minutes. Do you hear me, Veronica? Then we make our way back to a signal to call Chief Fanelli. You know it's the wisest thing to do."

Veronica came to an abrupt stop and turned on him. He could see tears in her eyes and knew she was frustrated. She placed her gloved hand on his chest, and he thought she would argue. But after a moment, all she did was nod once and turn back around to keep walking. "I just know we're so close."

"Then we'll come back out with a team and cover more ground. This park is huge. Too large for just the four of us. And with each step into the wilderness, we put our own lives at risk. We'll be no good to Jasmin if we succumb to the elements."

She picked up her steps and rushed forward.

"Did you hear me?" Parker raced ahead to keep up. "Veronica!" After having fallen through the snow, he would think she would be a little more careful on her footing.

"I see a cave! She had to have gone there." Veronica sunk deep into the snow with each step. Snow flew out as she plowed through.

Parker peered over her head and took note of a small opening in a crevice of the mountain. If nothing else, they would be able to get out of the cold. He wondered if Donovan would track them out here, knowing there would be no cell signal to call him. Parker had a feeling Veronica would use this cave as an excuse for not going back. She was a good cop, but she wasn't thinking clearly.

But then, this was about Jasmin. She was

one of them, and she deserved every effort to find her.

He felt so conflicted. For all he knew they were walking into an ambush. With each step they took as they neared the cave opening, he prepared himself to be shot at again. He surveyed the area and took note of the evergreens weighted down by heavy chunks of snow. They partially blocked the view of the full opening. He noticed two ways up to the cave. One route required them to walk up the slope. Going the other way meant going on the other side, on a more flattened landscape.

"I think it would be best if we split up. You take the higher entrance, and I'll come up the slope from below." Parker waited for Veronica's response as she kept moving forward with an obvious one-track mind. "Did you hear me?"

"Yes, but I don't agree. We're stronger in numbers. As soon as we reach the ledge, we'll untether ourselves. We'll treat this as any forced entrance. I go first, with you as my backup. Guns drawn."

"I would rather go first."

Veronica turned her head back. The look she sent him suggested she'd be unrelenting in her stance. Parker had no choice but to accept the plan as it was, and trust in her capabilities.

"You're the boss. We'll do it your way."

With that, they continued up the side to the left of the cave and walked carefully along a narrow path against the mountain. Even the dogs stayed close to the wall, so as not to fall off the ledge. When they reached the shadowed area of evergreens, Parker was glad to see Veronica slow her steps and ease around the corner. As soon as they cleared it, she unhooked their ropes and moved Summer to her side. She turned back and gave one nod, her gun already in her hand.

This maneuver had been an exercise they had practiced many times at headquarters. Most times, it was to enter a door or house. They never practiced entering a cave.

"Catch them by surprise. Be as loud as

you can be," he whispered, and at her nod, she stepped in with him right behind her.

They both yelled, "Police! Put your hands up!"

Bitter cold hit his face, but as far as he could see, the place was empty. Still, he dared not lower his weapon until he searched the opening thoroughly. The ground was slick with ice, but he could see no shadows for anyone to hide in.

"I think it's clear," he said. "Rosie, search." The dog sniffed around and quickly sat down to alert them that they were alone. At her notice, the two of them walked around the cave for any evidence left behind. He took out Jasmin's glove again and gave it to Summer. "Seek."

Summer went to work, hunting for any sign of Jasmin having been there. She quickly picked up the scent.

"She's been here," Veronica said quickly. "I knew it."

They followed Summer farther into the cave. With each step, the temperature lowered.

"We're in some sort of ice cave, I think,"

Parker said just as Rosie sat and whined. He kneeled to find something on the floor. As his hand made contact, he saw it was white and blended in with its surroundings.

"What is it?" Veronica crouched beside him. She inhaled sharply and reached for the item. "It's Jasmin's hat."

Parker withdrew a small flashlight from his waist pack. Shining the light on the hat, bloodstains showed up on the brim. It was a matching hat to Veronica's.

"I thought it would be cute to wear the same ski hats." The threat of tears could be heard in her voice, and Parker touched her back reassuringly.

"We'll find her." The blood pointed to Jasmin being injured, but he didn't have to tell Veronica that. They both knew the statistics of the chances of someone being alive with each passing hour.

She glanced farther into the dark cave. "We have to keep going. I can't go back now. She's in here somewhere, and she's hurt. I can't wait for backup."

"I know. I don't like it, but I understand. Consider me your backup."

The light beam caught Veronica's wide eyes studying him. "You really are a good friend." She touched the front of his coat. He wished he could feel her touch through the thick padding of the jacket. Still, his heart warmed with the sentiment.

"Always." A moment of appreciation passed between them before Parker took a deep breath and stepped back to remove his backpack. "We'll need our headlights."

Veronica followed his moves and retrieved her own gear, and soon they were moving deeper into the void. They walked for about ten minutes side by side with the dogs leading the way on their leashes. He found he liked having her there instead of behind or in front. It felt more personal, as if they were doing this together. A real team and not an obligation.

"I feel air blowing on us," she whispered, picking up her steps. "There must be an exit close by."

"The passage narrows ahead. Only one of us will fit at a time."

"I'm going first."

Parker wasn't about to negotiate. "Just

have your gun ready for whatever is on the other side."

She held it high for him to see, and then she fitted her body into the slim opening. Summer followed right behind her, then Rosie and him. The icy walls were slick as they passed through and all was quiet, except for the boots softly shuffling along the rough floor.

Suddenly, Veronica shouted, "Police! Drop your weapon!"

Before Parker could push through, a bang blasted through the cave, the loud crack bouncing off the walls and through his head.

"Veronica! Get back!" Parker yelled as he raced ahead to grab her. But when he burst through the narrow passage, it was Veronica holding the gun with a motionless man at her feet.

SEVEN

Veronica stood still, in complete shock, the weapon in her hand at the ready. "I…" She couldn't speak, even as Parker ran around her and kneeled by the body of the man she had shot. "Oh, Parker." Her voice trembled. "Did I kill him?"

He felt for a pulse and nodded. He then reached for the gun on the floor and pushed it away. "What happened?"

Veronica lowered her gun to her side and forced herself to go over the fast sequence of events. She knew it wouldn't be the first time she would have to retell them. What would Chief Fanelli do to her? "I stepped out of the passageway and saw the gun pointed at me. He started to shoot me, but I shot first. I didn't even hesitate. I think I'm going to be sick."

Parker stood and stepped in front of her. "It was self-defense. You would have been killed. No one will fault you."

Veronica looked around Parker to the man. "Is he the kidnapper?" She scanned the small space, looking for Jasmin. "If I killed him, I'll never know where my sister is. Oh, what was I thinking?" Her attention fell back on the body lying facedown.

"You were thinking you had to do whatever it took to stay alive." He held her upper arms. "Look at me."

Veronica peeled her gaze from the body, but wasn't really seeing Parker's face even with the headlamp shining on him. Her brain skewed her surroundings and made everything distant. She reached her free hand to grip his coat, as if to keep from collapsing. She still might. "I've never shot anyone before."

He shook his head. "And it won't be the last time either. You had no choice. You told him to drop his weapon."

"I did?" She wasn't even sure.

"Yes, I heard you loud and clear. You followed protocol, sweetheart." He pulled her close, and she rested her forehead on his shoulder. It took her a moment to realize he had called her a term of endearment. Ordinarily, she would have been irritated by it, but at this moment, it made her feel comforted. She wasn't going through this alone, or with someone who didn't care about her. Because Parker really did care about her. She supposed deep down she always knew he did. Perhaps more than a friend, as well.

Veronica pulled away, lifting her chin in determination. "We have to keep moving. We're close to finding Jasmin. This man wouldn't have been here otherwise."

"Do you want me to lead this time?" Parker asked.

Veronica agreed, but it wasn't much farther before they entered into another chamber, and as they cast their headlamps around the rocky room, a hunched-over figure sitting against the wall caught their beams.

"Jasmin!" Veronica raced around Parker and up to her sister.

Jasmin was sitting with her hands bound and her mouth gagged, and when Veronica moved close, her sister twisted to get away.

"It's me—Veronica. We're here to help you. Jasmin, do you hear me?" Veronica moved her headlamp off to the side so Jasmin could see her face clearly. Jasmin was trembling from the cold and, most likely, fear, but finally calmed enough to focus. She lurched toward Veronica, whining through her gag.

Veronica pulled down the gag and Jasmin immediately said, "You have to get out of here. It's not safe."

"I shot the guy. He's dead." Veronica untied the ropes at her wrists.

"Both of them?" Jasmin asked as Veronica removed her gloves and fitted them on Jasmin's bare hands.

"There's two?" Parker asked from behind, and at Jasmin's emphatic nod, he moved the dogs to stand guard. "Makes sense. When they shot Tyrese, someone had been driving."

"Tyrese?" Jasmin's voice turned more fearful than before. "Tyrese Turner?"

Veronica paused at the bindings on her sister's ankles and studied the fear in her shadowy face. "Yeah, why?"

"Tyrese is more dangerous than them all. Why would you contact him?"

Parker crouched and looked Veronica's way. His confused expression had to match her own.

"Jasmin," Veronica said carefully, unsure if her sister had been hit on the head. "We didn't contact him. You did. We saw your text to him."

Jasmin shook her head repeatedly. "Only if I had a death wish would I contact him. And if he's behind all this, then I'm dead already."

Parker guided the two women from the cave back the way they had come. Jasmin had been blindfolded and knocked out by her kidnapper, so she couldn't be sure how far another exit was. With Veronica holding her sister up in her weakened state, he thought it best to retrace their steps, even if it was a long way and they had to pass the deceased kidnapper. The way Veronica stared at the man as they went around him caused Parker to worry about her state of mind. He couldn't let her feel guilty over killing the man.

"Your quick response saved us all. Don't ever forget that." He touched her back and guided her through the narrow passage once again. "Your sister would have never been found. And, most likely, neither would we."

"I know. It doesn't make it any easier to accept, but I know."

As the passage opened up wider, Parker moved in front of them, his own gun ready in case the second kidnapper returned. In his other hand, he held tight to both of the dogs' leashes so Veronica could help her sister. When they reached the end of the passage, he commanded the K-9s to sit before exiting. He didn't want to alert the women, but he considered the rescue to be too easy. Why go to such great lengths to kidnap Jasmin and frame her for the murder of her sister if they were willing to let her go?

He scanned the next portion of the cave and it appeared empty, but there were many shadows his headlamp didn't reach. The second kidnapper could be in any one of them. He didn't want to put the dogs in danger first, but he saw no other way to assure their safety.

"Search," he commanded them, and let the K-9s take the lead. Within moments, the dogs began barking. Parker had been correct. They weren't alone in this cave.

In the next second, footsteps could be heard running toward the opening of the cave. Parker moved to go after them but slowed his steps when he realized the sisters weren't with him. As much as he wanted to go after the man, the women needed him to stay close. By the time they made it to the opening of the cave, there was no sign of the second kidnapper.

"We can't go back the way we came," Veronica said. "We could fall through, and Jasmin isn't strong enough."

Parker agreed and tried to remember the layout of the area from the last search he took part in when Chief Fanelli had sent him and Brandie Weller out here to help with a case.

"I think I remember another way to get

us to higher ground," he said. Studying Jasmin's weakened state, he worried that she could make the climb. "Are you up for it? We'll stop whenever you tell us to."

At her nod, he led the way back toward the cliff, but instead of staying low, he sought a higher elevation path. As soon as his phone picked up a signal, he made the call to Chief Fanelli.

"We have Jasmin," he informed their boss. "We had to take down one of the kidnappers. He's still in the cave." From there, he gave Donovan the directions he needed to meet them.

"I'll let the local police know. And I'll be speaking to the two of you for not waiting. But for now, I can have a chopper meet you to pick you up. The pilot will take Jasmin to a hospital to be assessed for injuries. Do either you or Veronica need medical attention?"

"No, sir. We're safe and the K-9s are safe."

"Great. What do you know about Tyrese Turner?"

Parker shot a look at Jasmin, then slowly asked, "What about him?"

"He's here with us now. Real concerned about Jasmin. I knew she had been married before she came on the team, but she has never spoken about him to me."

"There's a good reason." Parker lowered his voice and turned away from the women. "In fact, don't trust him. He could be involved."

"He says he took a shot. Are you sure?"

Parker wasn't sure about anything. "I can only go by what Jasmin said."

The helicopter could be heard approaching overhead.

"I'll keep him close and see what I can get out of him," Donovan said.

Parker watched the chopper hover above them and led the women to a clearing. "Our ride is here. We'll see you at the hospital."

"Will do. I'm glad it all worked out, and you're all safe. See you soon." Donovan ended the call just as the helicopter descended in front of them.

"Let's go!" Parker yelled and waved his arm for Veronica to lead her sister out. He kept his other hand on the dog's leashes and followed from behind as the women made their way toward the opened side door.

Parker saw the spark before he heard the sound. The noise of the rotating blades covered up the gunshots, but the hole in the side of the helicopter spoke loud enough.

They were being shot at.

"Go!" he shouted as loud as he could, pushing his free hand at Veronica's back and shielding her with his body. "They're shooting at us!"

The door to the helicopter now seemed so much farther away than a moment before. With the deep snow to slow them down, it took every ounce of strength to push forward.

Another bullet hit the snow and then the ground rumbled around them. As they reached the helicopter. Veronica lifted her sister up by the waist and hauled them both inside. Parker let the leashes go so the dogs could race ahead and jump in. When he jumped aboard, she pulled the door shut just as the snowy mountains cracked and huge chunks of snow fell in an avalanche.

The pilot lifted off the ground as snow

filled the clearing below. One more second, and they would have all been buried alive. The pilots sent back headsets for them to wear. Once they were in place, Jasmin spoke first.

"Tyrese did this," she said.

"That's impossible," Parker replied. "Donovan is with him right now. He can't be in two places at once."

"That's what I always thought too, but my ex-husband is full of surprises, and none of them are good."

EIGHT

In the quiet hospital room, Veronica sat next to her older sister's bed and observed her bandaged head and hands. The way the tables had turned felt unfamiliar to her, the younger sister. It had always been Jasmin caring for her, making sure she was safe and protected. But now Jasmin needed Veronica to take the reins.

"I want to be here for you like you have always been there for me, but, Jasmin, how can I do that when you kept me in the dark?"

Jasmin opened her eyes and reached one of her bandaged hands her way. She had serious frostbite, but thankfully her fingers and toes should heal.

"It wasn't about keeping things from you," Jasmin said weakly. "It was shame on my part. Embarrassment, really. I didn't want to admit to you that I allowed myself to be controlled by Tyrese."

Veronica hadn't been speaking about her marriage to Tyrese, although Jasmin's secrecy was adding up to be a pattern. "You didn't have to suffer alone. I could have been there for you."

"Oh, sweetie, you were enjoying your high-school years, going to prom and making friends. I doubted you would have even understood what I was going through. No. I had to handle my marriage and divorce alone. I had to find my own way out of it. And I did. Just not far enough away, I guess."

"You really think Tyrese is behind your kidnapping?" Veronica said in a low voice as she leaned forward. "He seemed so sincere. And he took a bullet meant for me."

Jasmin sighed and looked to the ceiling. "I suppose I could be wrong, but I just don't think I am."

Silence settled between them, but Veronica needed details. She needed to know the full truth if she was ever going to understand her sister's fear and choices.

"What happened between you and Tyrese? Tell me everything. I can handle it. You don't have to protect me anymore. I'm a cop now. I need to know."

Jasmin was still for so long, Veronica wondered if her pain meds had kicked in and knocked her out. But, finally, her sister spoke, and Veronica was sure she had never heard such pain in Jasmin's voice before.

Jasmin had always been a funny and cheerful person.

Had it all been a facade?

"I hid the bruises well," she said in a strained whisper.

Veronica held her shock in check. She needed to prove that she was mature enough for this conversation. "So it was physical, as well."

Jasmin nodded and tears welled up in her eyes. "I was so afraid. I was ashamed."

"It was not your fault," Veronica answered quickly.

"You don't understand. I brought this on myself."

"That's a lie. No one deserves to be mistreated or abused. If I had known, I could have done something."

"You're here for me now. That's all that matters."

"I am. And I'm going to find out who's behind your kidnapping too."

"And your attempted murder. Don't forget that." Jasmin's voice broke. "I'm so sorry you were brought into this."

"Into what?" Veronica demanded a little too harshly. But she needed answers. "What were you doing? Someone left a cryptic message on your voice mail at headquarters. Something about you being found. Were you hiding from someone?"

The door opened and Donovan stepped in with Parker. "You're awake. Good," the chief said, moving to the foot of the bed. "Glad to have you back with us. Can you talk?"

Chief Fanelli's laser focus worked for Veronica. Time was critical if they didn't want to lose the scent of whoever was behind the kidnapping and the fire.

Jasmin chewed her lower lip as the boss stared her down. Veronica felt a little bad for her big sister. Being under Chief Fanelli's scrutiny wasn't a comfortable place to be, especially after coming so close to death.

"Where's Tyrese?" Jasmin asked nervously.

"Down in the waiting room," Chief Fanelli replied.

She frowned. "Sir, I'm sorry to say, but in an attempt to protect myself, I may have brought this trouble on."

Donovan nodded once. "That's what I was afraid of. I will need all the details."

Jasmin nodded. After a few breaths, she said, "I broke into his house and safe and took $10,000."

Veronica inhaled sharply at her sister's confession, but quickly pressed her lips tight to keep from reacting further. She felt Parker's hand on her back, and somehow, the man's touch eased her tension even more. Veronica turned her head to offer him a slight smile of gratitude for being there for her through every twist and turn. She didn't know how she would ever make it up to him. He had gone above and beyond what she deserved. His reminder that she was already forgiven allowed her to ready herself to help her sister.

Veronica had a kidnapper and attempted murderer to track and apprehend.

"Go on," Donovan said to Jasmin.

"About a month ago, one of my investment accounts had been hacked. I lost ten thousand dollars in a second. I reported the money missing and closed that account, but... I guess I needed to know who breached the wall. It felt personal. So I looked into the investment company's server to see who had access that night. I found an IP address that had bypassed the security system. I then tracked the IP address to a location in Seattle. This wasn't an offshore hack. It was someone local. And I was the only one affected by it."

Veronica said, "The message on your voice mail. Who was that?"

"I don't want to get him into trouble, but his name is Elliot Dumas. He works in the IT department for the firm. He helped me figure out where the money was routed to. He warned me I could be inviting trouble to my doorstep. I thought he meant criminal charges, but I see now that he meant trouble from the dark side of the web. I found the location of the hacker, and that opened a whole other threat when he found me."

Veronica huffed. "And here I thought our Christmas ski weekend was a way to bond. You were hiding out."

"I'm sorry," Jasmin frowned. "I panicked, I guess. I didn't think anyone would find us out there in the woods. I thought a few days away would make them move on."

"Who's the hacker?" Donovan asked.

She looked down at her hands. "I tracked IP address to a location of a two-block radius. But..." Jasmin looked to Veronica. "I had my suspicions Tyrese was behind this."

"Your ex-husband?" Donovan's brow furrowed, and he removed his cell phone from his belt. He typed out a message on it. "I can go interrogate him right now. I have Colt staying with him in the waiting room. Colt accompanied me on the drive out here." Officer Colt Maxwell had been with the PNK9 for three years and had a specialty of searching for dead people with his bloodhound partner that was trained in cadaver detection. It appeared Donovan had prepared for the worst when he chose Colt to assist in the search for Jasmin. "If Turner is behind this, he had me fooled. He seemed genuinely worried about you."

Jasmin pursed her lips. "Worried that I figured out it was him who stole my money. The amount was the exact number from my divorce settlement five years ago. He took everything else from our marriage, claiming *I* was the abuser. I had just enough to get an apartment and a used car. But I was free. When my account was hacked and the money stolen, I wasn't going to go away quietly this time. Those days were over."

Veronica thought that the idea of her sister abusing someone was completely absurd, but a five-year-old verdict was the least of their problems. "I'd like to interview Turner," she said to Donovan.

"You're too close to this. I need clear heads."

"I understand, sir, and I will. I just need to see his face when we bring these allegations up. He lied to me about Jasmin texting him. What else will he lie about?"

"I'll allow it, but Parker goes with you, and I won't negotiate that."

Donovan's comment made Veronica realize her animosity toward Parker had been noticed by everyone. She had so many fences to mend.

"Actually, I would be honored to work with Parker."

Donovan glanced Parker's way with a questioning look. His gaze fell on Parker's hand, which was on her back, and his expression softened around the hard edges. "I'm glad to see the walls coming down among my team. It will only make us stronger."

"It already has, sir," Veronica replied, turning her head to Parker. "Officer Walsh is a great cop and partner."

Parker smiled brightly. "Right back at you."

"All right, you two head down to Maxwell in the waiting room. I'd like to talk with Jasmin for a few minutes. We'll be heading back to headquarters shortly. The doctor has released Jasmin in my care."

With those orders, Veronica filed out behind Parker. They made their way toward the elevators and down to the first floor. They stepped out to find the room empty. As they circled around, a banging sound could be heard down a hallway.

Veronica followed the noise.

"Careful," Parker said. "Something doesn't add up. Where would Colt take Turner without permission?"

"Let me out!" Colt's muffled voice came out through a closet door.

Veronica checked the handle but found it locked.

A nurse came out from an office. "What is going on out here?"

"Miss, do you have a key for this room?" Parker asked.

The nurse pulled out a key ring and located the correct one, then passed it over to Veronica. Once unlocked, Colt burst out the door.

"Where is he?" Colt demanded. "Where's Tyrese Turner?"

Parker asked, "What happened?"

Colt's reddened face expressed anger and shock. He touched the back of his head.

"That weasel knocked me out. And apparently stuffed me in there."

Veronica locked her eyes on Parker's. "Jasmin was right. Tyrese is behind her kidnapping."

A fiery anger flared in Parker's eyes. "And behind *your* attempted murder."

Veronica's throat went dry at the memory of that deadly blaze, purposely set to kill her and frame Jasmin. "We have to find him. Now."

Before she could take one step, Parker reached for her forearm. "One wrong move, and we will fall right into another trap."

While Veronica readied Jasmin to leave, Parker pulled Donovan off to the side to speak privately. "I'd like to stay behind and see if I can track Turner around here before heading back. I can be a decoy to make sure he doesn't know they've returned to Olympia just yet too."

Donovan nodded. "I can leave Colt to assist and get Jasmin and Veronica to headquarters myself."

Veronica narrowed her gaze at Parker

from where she was kneeling to put on Jasmin's boots. "What are the two of you talking about?" She stood and approached them. Parker expected her to refute the idea and braced himself.

"I'm staying behind to try and catch Turner before he realizes you and your sister are gone. He won't expect Jasmin to be released so soon and will be waiting for a second chance. You know I'm right."

"It's not about being right. I want to catch him just as much as you do, maybe more. He tried to kill me."

"And won't think twice about doing it again. You're in just as much danger. I want you at headquarters, where I don't have to worry about watching your back."

"And who will watch your back?"

Colt interjected with a smirk. "What am I?"

Veronica flashed heated eyes at both of them. "You search for dead bodies."

Colt huffed. "That's not all I do, and you know it."

Veronica pressed her lips tight, and Parker

knew she felt cornered. He reached for her forearm with a gentle touch.

"I'll be safe. But your worry flatters me. I never knew you cared." He knew his joke had fallen flat when pain filtered in her gaze. "I'm sorry. That was rude of me."

"I do," she said quickly and moved forward to rest her forehead on his shoulder.

The room fell into complete silence, but Parker didn't care what any of them thought. He reached a hand to the back of her head and tunneled his fingers into her thick, soft hair.

Parker took the moment to let all they had been through heal their friendship.

"This isn't over," he said. "It's just the beginning."

Veronica lifted her gaze to his. "Find him and get back to Olympia."

"That's the plan."

With that, Donovan arranged for an ambulance to move him and the women out of the hospital secretly. Parker and Colt waited for them to have a thirty-minute lead, then they left by the front entrance with Summer and Rosie.

"He'll be watching and waiting for the sisters," Parker said. "I give him about five minutes before he realizes we pulled a fast one."

"Less," Colt replied with a nod toward the back parking lot. "That blue sedan is moving too slow. In a few seconds, he'll peel out of here to head west with one thing on his mind. Murder. The man will be livid."

True enough, just when Parker made it to Donovan's SUV and let the dogs inside the rear door, the blue car sped past them.

"Time to move out," Parker shouted as Colt climbed behind the wheel, and Parker jumped into the passenger side. "Don't lose him!"

"Not a chance."

As Colt raced after the car, he put the sirens on, but Turner only drove faster.

"He's getting on the highway."

Just then, Parker watched the driver-side window roll down. It stopped halfway, and the barrel of a gun appeared, directed at them.

"Gun!" he shouted, retrieving his own and readying it to shoot.

The gun barrel flashed with two shots before Parker could roll down his window. The SUV took the first bullet in the grille. The second hit the front passenger-side tire. A large pop sent the car out of control and toward the curb.

Turner's car took the ramp to get on the highway, but with a flopping tire and steam lifting from the radiator, Colt had no choice but to pull over and call the state patrol for help.

Parker banged his hand on his knee because of how fast they'd lost him. He pressed in Donovan's number, and when his boss picked up, he said, "He got away and he's heading in your direction. Guard Veronica and Jasmine with your life. We'll get there as soon as we can."

"We're making good time. I'm bringing them right to headquarters. With our security system, it's the safest place for them."

Parker had no choice but to sit tight and wait for help, and pray Chief Fanelli would get Veronica and Jasmin back to headquarters in time.

NINE

The song "A Holly Jolly Christmas" tinkled faintly through the speakers at headquarters as Veronica helped her sister inside and to her office. Just a couple of days ago, they had rushed out of here to get on the road for their ski weekend. Now, so much had transpired and changed that neither of them had words to express their shocking experiences. They had both come so close to death. Veronica wished the events would have brought her closer to Jasmin, but instead, she found herself pitying her sister. Perhaps if Jasmin had confided in her from the beginning, Veronica could have cut off Tyrese before he'd put his plan in motion.

"I should've known he would retaliate," Jasmin said as she took a seat on her office sofa.

"When you saw your money missing, how did you know it was him?"

She shrugged. "I just did. He hated that I walked away with anything from our marriage. I knew eventually he would come for it. I just never expected him to hack into my account. I was so mad that he had bested me again. I had to see his face when I accused him of it."

"I can't believe you went to his house alone. What were you thinking?"

Jasmin looked at her computer on her desk and chewed on her lower lip. Slowly, she got to her feet and made her way around the desk. Sitting in an office chair, Veronica thought about all the times her sister had handled her position with maturity and wisdom. The whole unit depended on her for their success.

"I was thinking that I was not the same young woman he took advantage of. I was thinking that I would show him that, once and for all. When I got to the house, the house that used to be mine, I knocked but there was no answer. The door was unlocked, and I walked right in. It felt so surreal to be in there again like I never left. I went to the bedroom and found the safe. The code was easy to crack, and...there was the money. Ten thousand dollars." Jasmin lifted her chin. "I took it back." Her answer was swift and defiant.

Veronica felt her mouth fall open. "I can't believe you broke the code on his safe."

Jasmin fell back into her desk chair and slouched. "You don't understand. Tyrese controlled everything. What I wore. Who I hung out with. How much money I was allowed to have. I couldn't let him get away with this. I had to show him that I couldn't be controlled anymore."

Jasmin glanced up, and Veronica never saw her sister look so forlorn. But then she saw a twinkle in her eye and a wisp of a smile spread across her face, as if she was remembering something that only she could see.

"Do you know why I became a computer technician?" Jasmin asked.

Veronica honestly had no idea what the answer was to her sister's question. It only proved how distant they were. "I just assumed it was something you were interested in."

Jasmin shook her head. "He was tracking me. My every move was always accounted for. I investigated how to bypass his system, and I learned how to hack into it." Her smile grew brighter. "I remember the first time I went somewhere without him having any idea that I'd even left the house. I felt so free." She lifted her chin. "I'm not sorry for it."

Veronica shook her head. "You shouldn't be." She weighed her next words carefully. "I'd have to think that made him very angry to see you outsmart him. Not only with the tracking, but also with taking the money back. Enough to ruin you by framing you for murder and then making you disappear forever. But I have to ask you something."

"What?"

"You said there was exactly ten thousand dollars in the safe, right?"

"Yes, why?"

"And the front door was unlocked?"

Jasmin nodded slowly.

"Big sister, I hate to tell you this, but it

sure looks like you played right into his sick and twisted hands again."

Jasmin dropped her head back on the cushioned chair. "You're probably right. But I just couldn't let him get away with it," she said in a soft whisper.

Veronica frowned, feeling sorry for all her sister endured with this man. "He won't. Donovan's bringing in a few other officers and they will cut him off at the highway before he ever exits. They'll catch him."

The visible sigh escaping from Jasmin's lips proved the stress and fear this man had caused her sister. Veronica headed to her locker to get her own gun. If Tyrese made it past Donovan's barricade and into the PNK9 unit, she would be ready to stand between him and Jasmin.

As she walked back toward Jasmin's office, she passed the half-decorated Christmas tree. With everyone so busy with their caseloads and their own holiday preparations, no one had had time to finish dressing the tree.

"How about hanging some ornaments with me?" she asked Jasmin, thinking it would take her mind off the threat for a few minutes.

"I suppose a little mindless decorating would ease my tension." Jasmin stood carefully and made her way out into the hall. "Sitting and waiting won't make the time go faster."

The two of them began opening the boxes under the hall table. Veronica noticed yesterday's newspaper still sitting with the office mail. The front page showcased the big Christmas parade coming up in Emeryton between Christmas and New Year's Eve.

"It's so weird how one event can ruin the whole season," Veronica said, returning with a box of lights. "I don't even feel like celebrating the holidays now. I just want to go home and lock the doors behind me."

"I'm sorry," Jasmin said. She picked up some tinsel. "Do you remember how Mom hated this stuff?"

Veronica cracked a smile. "She was finding the stuff for months after Christmas. Always vowing to never use it again."

"And yet, she still does to this day."

"Yeah, but we're not there to throw it at

each other." Veronica picked up a handful and threw it in Jasmin's hair. Before she knew it, she was also picking the silver strands out of her own hair. "Just like old times."

"You were such an annoying little sister," Jasmin teased.

"And you were always complaining about me to Daddy." Veronica stuck out her tongue but couldn't suppress her smile for long.

"Well, Daddy did like me better."

"No way, not a chance." Veronica threw more tinsel, and soon, Jasmin had tears in her eyes. "Hey, I didn't mean to hurt you."

Jasmin turned back to her office, waving Veronica away. "I'm fine. I just need a minute. Just talking about Daddy made me miss him."

Veronica followed her sister back to the couch, but she sat on the opposite end, on the edge. "I wish he was still with us too." Their father had passed away in Veronica's senior year of college. "And I'm sure you were his favorite."

Jasmin shook her head. "I was just kidding. He loved us both, and this whole thing would devastate him. I'm glad he's not here to see it."

"He would protect us."

Jasmin smiled. "Yes, he would. But speaking of protecting… What's going on with you and Parker? I've never seen the two of you so close. Not even when you were friends."

This was not a conversation that Veronica was ready to have. She didn't have an answer that even made sense to her. She stood to return to the tree and her box of lights. Scooping a mangled mess of stringed lights, she went to work of detangling them, all while avoiding the question.

"I take it you don't want to talk about it," Jasmin called from her couch.

"We're friends again. Can't that be enough?"

"You tell me. Would that make you both happy? Or is there a part of you that wants more?"

Veronica shook out the strand, finally free of knots. It was a satisfying victory, and she found herself wishing Parker was here to help decorate the tree.

"I think I want more. When we were both candidates, I enjoyed his company. He was so conceited, but I still trusted him to have my back. Then all the sabotage that made him look guilty only made me doubt my instinct as a cop. Maybe that's why it took me so long to forgive myself."

"But you were right about him from the beginning. It was everyone else who was wrong. You saw something in him the rest of us missed. He's blessed to have a friend like you. And judging by the way he held you in my hospital room, he wants more than friendship too."

Veronica felt her cheeks flush at the thought. She turned around to wrap the strand around the tree, starting at the top and circling around the back of the pine. As soon as she stepped out of Jasmin's line of view, she caught a movement off to her left. But before she could say anything, Tyrese stepped around the corner and reached for the strand of lights with lightning speed. The next second, he wrapped the strand around Veronica's neck while she grasped at the tightening plastic that was cutting off her air.

Tyrese shoved her out from behind the tree. "Look what I have here, Jasmin," he taunted as he yanked the cord tighter.

Veronica choked and felt her head go light. She struggled to reach behind her, but Tyrese pulled an arm around and pinned down her arms. With her eyes blurring, she couldn't see her sister.

"Let her go! She's innocent in all this," Jasmin pleaded. "I'll give you the money back."

Tyrese laughed in Veronica's ear. His hot breath hit her cheek. "I'll need more than that now." He yanked the cord tighter, and Veronica felt her limbs go weak and her eyes bulge. She was being asphyxiated. She didn't know how much longer she could hang on. He was squeezing her neck so tight. "In case you didn't notice, I'm pulling the strings, and now, you're going to do exactly as I say. Or your baby sister is dead. Do you understand?"

Jasmin raced toward her, her eyes wide

in fright. "Please let her go. You're killing her."

"Exactly. If you want this to end well, you'll follow my orders to a *T*."

Veronica tried to shake her head to tell her sister not to obey Tyrese. But if Jasmin noticed, she didn't listen.

"Please don't kill her. I'll do whatever you say. Just please don't kill her. What do you want?"

"We're going to our getaway. But first, you're going to return my money. Every last cent. Then maybe, I'll let your sister go."

Veronica couldn't keep her eyes open anymore. As her body went limp, she accepted that Tyrese wouldn't be keeping any bargains.

The SUV's radiator steamed the whole way back, but at least Parker and Colt were able to change the tire to the spare and get back on the road. As they pulled up to the exit for headquarters, Colt stopped at the barricade Donovan had set up.

Parker jumped from the passenger seat with his gaze fixed on his boss, who was among the troopers in their winter parkas. "Please tell me you cut Turner off by now." The cold turned his own air to steam.

"There's been no sign of the make and model of his car."

Parker rubbed his forehead and turned to the oncoming traffic that was slowly driving by the single-lane checkpoint. "He must have taken another route."

"State patrol has checkpoints at all the other routes. No one has seen him come through yet."

"This isn't right. I feel it in my gut that he's already skirted through. I don't know how, but he played us." He headed toward the lined-up cruisers that blocked the highway traffic from avoiding the checkpoint. "I need a car! I'm going to headquarters."

"Take the last one on the right," Donovan ordered, lifting his phone to his ear. "I'll check in with Veronica."

When Parker backed the cruiser out of the line, he glanced back to see his boss waving him to go. The look on Donovan's face was loud and clear. Veronica wasn't answering.

Parker flipped on the siren and the lights, and raced toward the PNK9 Unit, speeding past cars that were pulled over and slipping around vehicles that weren't fast enough to move to the roadside. By the time he pulled into the parking garage, he noticed the garage door had been left open. It would only be open if someone had forced it open. Most likely, Turner had hacked the system and gained access.

Parker screeched the vehicle to a stop on the garage cement and barreled toward the entrance. Bursting through, he hustled to the office space. Christmas music played through the halls, a rendition of "Jingle Bell Rock." He skidded to a stop at the sight of a gun on the floor.

"Veronica!" he called as he picked it and placed it in his belt at his back. He retrieved his own and held it out in front of him.

No response came, and he moved forward to the offices. The lights were all on, so to avoid being seen, he stayed close to the wall and slid toward the opened door of Jasmin's office.

"Police!" he shouted and whipped around to breach the room.

The empty room.

Turning back, he searched the premises in the same fashion, only to come up empty.

The women were gone.

Taken. To only God knew where.

Parker called out to Him in this moment of fear and uncertainty. "You have never failed me. Your hand has guided my every step in life. I beg of You to move me in the right direction again. Lead me to… Veronica." Parker's voice cracked as he realized this wasn't just a prayer for her safety. It was a prayer for the woman of his heart.

The woman his heart belonged to…and he supposed always had.

Their early days as candidates had brought them together as friends, and so many factors had torn them apart. But he'd never stopped caring about her.

And I won't let this latest attempt to separate us be successful.

Parker moved to the back, where the kennels were. He located Summer and Rosie's chamber and let them out. After leashing them, he returned to Jasmin's office and found the coat that Veronica had worn that day.

Putting the coat under Summer's nose, he commanded, "Seek."

The K-9 went to work, sniffing the floor over to the tree. Parker noticed evidence of a struggle with a knocked-over box of ornaments and strewn tinsel. A strand of lights was also lying on the floor. The dog continued toward the main entrance, which was for public use.

So Turner had taken them out the front door.

Parker opened the door and gave Summer the lead. From there, she strained forward to rush ahead, moving around the back of the building. But when she came to a stop and sat on her haunches, Parker wondered how the women could just vanish from the lot.

Then he saw the tire tracks in the snow. A car had been here. If he read them right, they were heading north when they left. But to where? Finding Veronica and Jasmin in an unknown car would be impossible.

No, not impossible, he reminded himself. Nothing was impossible with Jesus.

And cameras.

Parker glanced up at the building for the cameras that could tell him the model of the car and the direction it had gone. He noticed it on the corner of the roof.

"Thank You, God, for guiding me. Keep leading me in the way I should go. Make my paths straight to Veronica. Straight to the woman who has my heart. My friend who is so much than a friend."

So much more.

As Parker headed back inside, he remembered the pain he felt when Veronica had turned her back on him and their friendship. He did forgive her, but the pain was still there under the surface. Losing her once was hard enough. He couldn't lose her again.

He wouldn't.

Back inside, he commanded the dogs to sit by the sofa in Jasmin's office, while he went to her desk to see if he could log in to view the recordings.

Where would Turner take them? His

home? Was the man stupid enough? Parker doubted it, but he would do a search on Turner's place of residence too.

When he woke up the mouse, the screen displayed the website of a bank. The message on the screen stated Jasmin had timed out, so he couldn't see what she had been doing, but he figured that this might be the place Turner was taking them.

Parker decided the bank would be the first place to search. He would trust God for the next one, but hoped he wouldn't need one.

TEN

"Do you have the money you owe me?" Tyrese said through the cell phone's speaker. Veronica held the phone while Jasmin settled behind the car's wheel. They drove the stolen car that Tyrese had taken to get past the checkpoint unnoticed. He was driving one of PNK9's cruisers from the garage and had followed from directly behind so he could watch them carry out his orders.

"Yes, it's all here," Jasmin said, holding the bank envelope of cash. "Even though I don't owe you anything."

"Get used to it," he said. "You'll be owing me for the rest of your life. It's up to you how long that will last."

Veronica shook her head at her sister to keep her from saying anything else. The searing pain in her throat led her to consider her words carefully. She had underestimated Tyrese's vengeance. This went beyond marital retaliation. Tyrese had never meant to let Jasmin go. Even unto death. But she also knew, he had no use for her and would dispose of her as soon as he had his money, and his wife.

But Veronica wouldn't be leaving Jasmin, no matter what.

Veronica looked in her side mirror to see Tyrese. He had on sunglasses and a PNK9 cap. To anyone walking by, he looked the part. To her, he would never be worthy to wear the uniform. To think the man went to such lengths for ten thousand dollars astounded her, but then his motives went beyond money.

She glanced her sister's way and the myriad of emotions on her face as she also looked into the rearview mirror flitted from fear to anger and back to fear. Tyrese's motive wasn't about the money at all. It was a power grab, and Veronica would die before she allowed the man to prove his dominance over Jasmin.

"You got away before," Veronica whispered so Tyrese wouldn't hear. "You can do it again."

Jasmin shot her a wide-eyed look, shaking her head. Was she giving up already?

Jasmin's gaze fell on the markings on Veronica's neck, and in that moment, Veronica knew her sister was wavering.

"Don't go there," Veronica warned in a low voice. "You don't have to protect me anymore. You don't have to hide your pain from me."

"You still have so much to live. Go— run. It's me he wants." Jasmin whispered and jutted her chin toward the door. "Get out now."

"I'm not leaving you."

"You're right. I'm leaving you." Jasmin's voice grew louder. "Now go." The authoritative tone in her big sister's voice was the sister she knew. But now, Veronica knew Jasmin had hidden behind false bravery for a long time. Inside, she was a frightened young woman who'd also given up many years of living.

All because of the man behind them, who had control of her every move.

"Please, let me help you." Veronica knew Tyrese could hear them now, but she didn't care.

"You'll help me by getting out of this car. Run. He'll chase me before he chases you. It's the only way, and you know it. He'll kill you just as easily as he set the fire to kill you the first time. You are disposable to him, but you're not to me. You're everything to me." The sad smile on her sister's lips cut Veronica to her core. "You were always so much stronger than me."

"I always thought the same about you. I wanted to grow up to be just like you."

"No. You're perfect the way you are," Jasmin said loudly.

Tyrese scoffed through the phone's speaker. "Enough. No one's going anywhere. I'll shoot before you take two steps out the door. I'm in uniform. And you're in a stolen car. No one will try to stop me."

Veronica nodded to her sister. The risk was too great. "Together. We'll do this together."

"How sweet." Tyrese's snide comment nearly made Veronica jump from the car just to put him in his place. But getting herself shot and killed wouldn't help Jasmin. She needed to keep a level head.

"Just tell us what you want," Veronica said as she bit her tongue.

"Good girl. Jasmin could take a lesson of obedience from you."

"It's not obedience if there's coercion." She thought of Parker's obedience to God, and how it came willingly. Parker would be the first person to say God was a gentleman and would never force someone to comply against their will.

"You haven't seen anything yet," Tyrese warned. "You're about to find out just how persuading I can be. It will be up to you how much pain I will have to inflict. Right, Jasmin? Tell your sister how it doesn't have to hurt too much. Just follow every word exactly as I say, and the pain won't be so bad."

Veronica watched her sister's fingers curl around the steering wheel in a death grip. The way she trembled told Veronica that Jasmin had given up. For her strong sister to succumb to Tyrese's demands, she must believe that there's no hope.

"Stay with me," Veronica whispered, reaching to put her hand on her thigh.

As Jasmin turned to face her, her eyes filled with tears. "I'm going to get you out of this."

Before Veronica could reply, Jasmin faced forward and floored the gas pedal, shooting the car forward with a loud screech.

"Where do you think you're going?" Tyrese yelled through the phone. "Jasmin! You'll pay for this!"

Jasmin reached for the phone and Veronica's hand and hit the end-call button.

"What are you going to do?" Veronica asked.

"Just what I said. I'm going to get you out of this." She took the next right and an immediate left. After glancing in the rearview mirror, she took another right. She brought the car to an abrupt stop. "Get out."

Veronica shook her head. "I told you. I'm not going anywhere. We'll do this together."

In the most lethal tone Veronica at ever

heard her speak sister speak, Jasmin replied. "Get…out."

In that instant, the big sister took over, reminding Veronica of her place as the little sister. "Please. Let me help you. I should have been there for you during your marriage. Let me help you now."

A heavy, angry silence settled between them, giving Veronica no choice but to comply. She pulled the door handle and pushed the door wide to step out. Before she even had a chance to close the door, Jasmin sped off, causing the door to slam. She took the next right and disappeared, leaving nothing but the fading sound of her racing car in the distance.

Stunned, Veronica glanced around at her surroundings. Her sister had left her in an industrial park with empty parking lots. She made her way over to a large dumpster just as she saw Tyrese's stolen PNK9 car fly by in the same direction Jasmin had gone. Her sister's plan had worked. She had secured Veronica's safety, but only at her own sacrifice. But then, isn't that what Jasmin had always been doing? Suffering in silence to save anyone else from being caught in Tyrese's crosshairs.

Veronica made her way back out to the main road just as another black SUV cruiser came her way. Its tires screeched as the driver brought the car to a halt in front of her.

Parker was at the wheel. The dogs lifted their heads from the back in their cages. When Parker started to exit the car, she raced to the passenger side and opened the door to climb in.

"We have to go. Now! We have to catch Jasmin before Tyrese does."

"Where are they heading?"

Veronica realized her sister had shut the phone off before Tyrese could give them the next destination. She felt her shoulders slump as she dropped her face into her hands.

"I have no idea."

The complete look of devastation on Veronica's face cut Parker deep. Her beautiful eyes implored him to help her find her sister. He hadn't seen the car Jasmin had been driving. All he had seen was the PNK9 cruiser speed off at the bank. He had hoped the women were in it. Seeing Veronica on the side of the road had shocked him, but now here she was without Jasmin. Veronica had given him the make and model of the car Jasmin was driving, and he put out an APB on it. But with no clue as to where she was headed, he felt helpless once again.

Then he thought of how God had led him straight to her. It had to be God. In a city this size, there was no other explanation than God's hand upon them.

"Veronica, look at me." Parker reached for her chin and lifted her face to his. "We will find her. God hasn't let us down yet. He's been with us the whole time."

She covered his hand on her cheek and implored him with a glimpse of hope in her eyes. "Do you really believe that?"

"With all my heart. I'm a changed man because of Jesus. Anything is possible with Him. All someone has to do is look at me and see how much I have changed. It's all His doing. I'm just along for the ride. And He is with us now."

Her eyes drifted closed with a sigh. Her face leaned into his hand, and Parker moved to rest his forehead on hers. The touch felt natural, but when she didn't pull away, he felt the remaining barriers between them crumble away and found himself hoping that this meant she could believe in them too.

"What were some of the things Tyrese mentioned?" Parker asked without pulling back. "Did he mention a destination or some place of significance?"

"He never got that far. Jasmin disconnected and took off before he could. She kicked me out of the car." Veronica lifted her face to stare into his eyes. "In her attempt to save me, she signed her own death certificate."

"Jasmin is a smart woman. She knew what she was doing. And so do you. You're a great cop. I know this is personal, but I need you to step back from it and handle the situation as you would any case. With strength and being clearheaded. Can you do that, Veronica?"

Her eyes softened and relaxed. "Have I told you how amazing you are?"

Parker wasn't looking for an ego boost. He needed her to remember who she was. He needed her free from the clutches of fear. "No, but I'm only being a good friend."

"Just a friend?" Her head tilted. "Aren't we past that? Weren't we always?"

The question hung between them. And it seemed to be what she needed to push forward. Maybe it was what he needed too. He needed her to know he cared about her...as more than a friend. "I suppose we were... We are."

She nodded with a frown. "I'm so sorry. I let you down."

"No, sweetie." He cupped both her cheeks. "How could you know? The evidence against me put me in a bad light. You did what any good cop would do. You trusted the evidence."

"I should have trusted you."

"Do you now?"

"Yes. One hundred percent."

"Then that's all that matters. Okay? The past is forgotten. You don't have to ever bring it up. I won't even know what you're talking about." He cracked a smile.

In the next second, Veronica leaned forward and slammed into his lips on a rush. It didn't feel passionate, but more like a seal to close their past for good.

Sealed with a kiss.

As Parker realized his dream was coming true, and this woman who had his heart was giving him hers, he relaxed in the glory of her finally in his arms.

He never thought it was possible, but he was kissing Veronica Eastwood.

Joy swelled in Parker's chest, and more than ever, he had to be the best partner a cop could want. He had to be the best life partner a woman could need.

As much as he would love to continue kissing Veronica, time was critical. He forced himself to pull his lips away from hers, but he kept his hands on her cheeks. "We will explore this more, I promise. But right now, I need you to think if Tyrese mentioned any place at any time when you were with him. Even if it was spoken off the cuff."

Her eyes widened and she nodded quickly. "Yes. Back at the department, he had mentioned a place. I had forgotten about it because he had been choking me at the time."

Parker felt his stomach tighten, as if her words had kicked him in the gut. Another thing he would explore at a later time, particularly with Tyrese himself.

"Go on," Parker said. "What did he say?"

"He mentioned they were going home. Back to the place she never should have left. Their getaway. They had a seasonal property when they were married. He got it in the divorce. He got everything."

"Where is it?"

"Lake Quinault."

Parker released her and faced forward to take the wheel. It was hard to let her go, but he wouldn't let her down.

ELEVEN

The mix of emotions surging through Veronica had her gripping her midriff as Parker sped out of Olympia and through Aberdeen. Elation collided with anxiety, and anxiety fought with her attempt to remain focused.

Even an hour later, her lips still tingled from where they had sought comfort from Parker. *Who was she kidding?* Comfort wasn't the only thing Parker could offer her. And comfort wasn't really what she was looking for either.

Then what did she seek from him?

Love?

Veronica glanced out of the corner of her eyes to see the intense concentration on his face. He held nothing back as he raced to catch Tyrese before he hurt Jasmin.

"Keep an eye out for the car she's driving," he said, ending the long silent car ride as he headed north and moved closer to the lake and the western side of Olympic National Forest. "I hate to radio Donovan of our plans in case Turner is listening in. Can you call the chief?" He passed her his phone.

When Chief Fanelli answered, she filled him in and asked, "Could you arrange for backup on the eastern side of the lake? That's where their cabin had been."

"Theo is staying close to Willow right now as she nears her due date, but they live up near the park. I'll see if he is able to get involved."

"Let's just hope she doesn't go into labor in the meantime. The two of them have been through so much. I hate to call him out when Willow needs him most."

"Theo would be angry if anything happens to any of you and he wasn't called."

Veronica had to agree with the chief's statement. "I suppose I would feel the same way if one of our own was in this situation." Veronica gave the address to Donovan before disconnecting. It could be a while before Theo could get there. They may not be able to wait.

Finally, after another painful thirty minutes of driving across slick forest roads, the entrance to the lake area appeared up ahead. They passed by the Lake Quinault Lodge, with its festive Christmas decorations and lights. A huge brightly lit evergreen filled the large window. The welcoming sight should have brought her the peace of the season, but Veronica doubted there would be a Christmas for her this year if Jasmin wasn't alive to celebrate with her.

As they passed by the lodge, she mumbled, "It doesn't feel like Christmas."

"It's early still. Don't lose hope just yet. We'll find her, and you'll have something special to celebrate this year."

Veronica glanced Parker's way and thought about how she was already staring at that something special. "I'll try to remember that on Christmas morning. Thank you," she whispered and faced forward to build up her resolve as they neared the cabin.

"Do I take this next right?" Parker asked in the quiet cabin of the SUV. Even the dogs in the back were laying low in their individual cages. The heavy tension weighed on them all.

"The road after. Their cabin was closer to the back of the lake. If I remember correctly. It's been so long."

Lake Quinault sat on the Olympic Peninsula in the glacial-carved Quinault Valley at the southern edge of Olympic National Park's rainforest. The cold, wet climate made for traveling at a fast speed difficult, but Parker didn't seem too worried. At the turn, he slowed on a narrow side street that abutted the nearly frozen lake down a short embankment.

"Someone's been here recently. There are tire tracks on the pavement that the rain hasn't washed out yet."

"Only one set," Veronica said, hearing the hope in her voice. "Maybe Jasmin got away from him and she's not here."

"Or we're walking into a trap." Parker's heavy tone hit her with guilt. He removed a gun from the glove compartment and passed it to her.

Veronica frowned and stared at the weapon. "You're right. I *am* too close to this case. You should wait for Theo. I'd probably get us both killed."

Parker reached for her hand, pulling it close to him. "I didn't say that you should bow out. The fact that you recognize this now shows me you'll be smart about this. You had said you trust me. Well, I trust you too."

Veronica let out a pent-up breath. She didn't even know they were the words she needed to hear from him. Yes, she had told him she trusted him completely, but deep down, it was Parker who had the right to distrust *her.* She was the one who'd let him down.

But he *did* trust her.

"Thank you, Parker, for this amazing gift. And I don't mean the gun."

He flashed her a bright smile and winked in his sweet and charming way, not in arrogance at all. "Consider it an early Christmas gift. The first of many."

"Many?"

"Yes. Many gifts…over many years." His voice dropped low, and his sweet smile turned serious as his words stilled her loudly beating heart. "You didn't think I would be letting you go anytime soon, did you?"

His words should have raised her concerns, but instead, they only calmed her nerves. Somehow, Veronica found strength and peace in them.

"I don't want you to let me go." A laugh bubbled up to the surface, and she pulled his lips to hers for quick kiss. She whispered, "I'm so glad you're with me through this. I'm so glad you didn't let me push you away when Jasmin first went missing. You were the person I needed in this." She kissed his hand again. "And the person I need beside me…always."

Parker leaned in to kiss her, but before he made it halfway, the car jolted forward with a loud bang and crunch. They both flew forward before realizing they were being pushed down the embankment toward the icy body of water.

"Parker!" Veronica looked behind them. Out the back window, she saw Tyrese at the wheel of a truck. The lethal glare in the man's eyes suggested he meant to kill them both and wouldn't stop until he succeeded. "It's Tyrese. We have to get out of this car. He's pushing us in."

She readied her gun. They had a second to get out before they hit the water.

But the dogs were in the back!

Veronica unbuckled her seat belt and twisted around to get on her knees. She lifted her gun and took aim at the back window of the SUV. Three shots broke through the glass and into the windshield of Tyrese's car.

The dogs barked loudly from their cages.

"I can't take my foot off the brake! Can you release them from the cages?" Parker shouted.

Veronica climbed over the two sets of seats until she reached the back of the SUV. There she caught the satisfied expression on Tyrese's face in his vehicle. The man would not stop until he had pushed them into the lake.

Between the dogs' barking, the squealing of tires and the crunching of the two cars grinding together, the sounds were deafening and disturbing as Veronica attempted to free the animals.

"We're going in!" Parker shouted again.

The cacophony intensified with the splash of the SUV entering the lake in a plunge. Veronica screamed as the vehicle tilted on its rear and icy water rushed through the blown-out back window.

"Veronica! You need to get out now!" Parker grabbed hold of her leg and yanked her back.

"Not without the dogs! I won't leave them trapped." She expected Parker to speak reason and tell her they needed to leave them behind. But in the next second, he crawled over the front seat to assist her in reaching the latches.

Water sloshed all around them and continued to fill up the vehicle. It reached her shoulders, cutting her with its freezing temperatures. Her teeth chattered and her limbs slowed, but she still held tight to her weapon in her right hand.

Both she and Parker stood on the seat and pushed through the rushing water at the back to crawl across the cages. She felt her way with her free hand as her whole face was submerged.

Her fingers fumbled for the latch, but the air in the lungs dispersed too quickly. Pulling back, she stood to find an air pocket in sheer panic. Finally finding one, she refilled her lungs with a few panicked gulps and then dove back into the torrent. She hoped Parker wasn't having any trouble finding the other latch. She pushed through once again, holding her breath, laser-focused on her memory of the exact location of the handle. This time, her fingers made contact and she lifted the latch with ease. She pulled the cage door as wide as she could and hoped it would be enough for the K-9 to squeeze out.

But the dog didn't move.

She didn't know which dog she had, Summer or Rosie, but she figured they were both petrified at being submerged. She could only hope they were still alive as she reached a hand inside and yelled through the water with her last breath.

"Go!"

Her fingers gripped fur and the collar. She yanked the dog out. The animal strained but pushed through the grate and leaped out the blown-out back window. With no more air in her lungs, Veronica followed the dog out and swam up to the surface. Sunlight beckoned and seemed to be so close. But each stroke left her far below.

She watched the dog break through, and Veronica had to find solace in the fact that she was able to save at least one of them. She hoped Parker and his K-9 had escaped in time, but as her lungs squeezed in pain, and her eyes closed to darkness, Veronica had no choice but to accept her own demise.

Parker followed Veronica to the surface, but when he saw her let go of her gun and her arms go limp, he knew she had no fight left in her. Time was critical in saving her.

Her gun drifted down to him, and he grabbed it as he pushed harder to reach her and push her toward the surface. He broke through at the same time as Rosie and lifted Veronica's face out of the water. Summer swam through the freezing water toward shore as Tyrese's car backed up the embankment.

"Stay with me, Veronica," Parker said into his sweet love's ear with his gaze set on the shoreline. His voice trembled from the frigid temperature, but also because he realized that there was no denying his love for this woman. He had seconds to get them all out of the deadly situation, or they would have no future together.

He also had seconds to stop Tyrese from escaping, or the man would continue to be a threat to them all.

Parker knew he had to end this right here and right now.

Placing his cheek against Veronica's, he swam forward, jostling her to try to wake her up. He tilted her on her side to face him in an attempt to expel water from her lungs. He hoped he was in time before any damage could occur to her brain. With her lips near his, he gave her two breaths, and in the next second, she choked and water erupted from her.

Instantly, Veronica's arms flailed in her attempt to save herself.

"You're okay," Parker assured her. "Stay calm, and I'll get you out of the water."

"Parker," she said as her eyes adjusted on him. "The dogs?"

He smiled at her and loved her more in that instant. "Why am I not surprised your first concern would be for their safety? They are fine. Look." He turned her as he swam to shore, and his feet touched the ground. Both dogs were now shaking the cold water from their fur.

"Tyrese is getting away," she said. She pushed against him, wanting to stand on her own feet, but he wasn't sure she was strong enough. "We have to stop him."

"We will. I promise. But right now, I need to know that you're all right."

Veronica looked back at him and reached for his cheek. "I am, because of you. Thank you, Parker." The coloring was returning to her lips, and he felt it was safe enough to put her down and let her walk the rest of the way. After a few wobbly steps, he handed her gun to her. She took it gratefully and checked the chamber.

Parker ran up the embankment and after Tyrese's escaping car. He removed his own gun and took aim the back of the car. Veronica stood beside him with her own gun at the ready. Together, they blasted off four shots, blowing out the back tires and window of the car.

Tyrese continued down the lane, but the vehicle quickly came to an abrupt stop. As Parker and Veronica neared his car, they saw another car facing Tyrese and blocking the road.

"Jasmin!" Veronica raced ahead before Parker could stop her.

Tyrese stepped from the driver's side and had a gun in his own hand. He took aim at the driver blocking him.

"No!" Veronica shouted and barreled toward the man.

"Stop!" Jasmin yelled as she too climbed out from behind the wheel. She held up an envelope. "This is what you want. Your stolen money. Take it and leave us alone."

"It's too late for that, my dear," Tyrese said as he cocked the gun.

In the next second, Jasmin ran for the lake, and before anyone knew what she'd planned, she threw the money into the water.

"You're going to regret that," Tyrese shouted and took off around the front of his car to retrieve the cash. He ran into the water, diving to reach the sinking envelope. By the time he resurfaced, Summer and Rosie sat on the edge of the water waiting for him to return.

A car door slammed in the distance, and FBI agent Theo Bates appeared around the cars. "Sorry I'm late for the fun. I had to make sure Willow was with her mother before I could leave her. Although, it looks like you've got everything under control here. Shall I do the honors?" He removed his handcuffs from his belt.

The husband of PNK9 officer Willow Bates and soon-to-be father of their unborn child was an FBI profiler and special agent who specialized in serial bombers. But that didn't mean he couldn't help them out in a time of need.

Parker let out a deep sigh of relief. "You're just in time." He felt secure that this would be the end of the road for Tyrese.

As the man emerged from the frigid water, Parker expected him to freeze at the sight of the law waiting for him. Instead, he emerged with guns blazing.

The first shot was aimed right at Veronica. As she fell onto the ground, Parker's relief turned to horror. The only end of the road was Veronica's.

TWELVE

Veronica knew the bullet had come her way. She waited for the pain of torn flesh to debilitate her. With no vest to protect her, the bullet could penetrate anywhere on her body.

Except, the pain never came.

As she realized she felt nothing, Parker's face came into view above her. In a daze, she watched him assess her from head to toe. He looked frantic until his attention rested on her face.

"Did he miss?" Veronica asked.

A slow smile spread on Parker's face. "I think so." He helped her up to sit and as they both turned to the water, they found Jasmin struggling with Tyrese and Theo racing in the water to apprehend the man.

The dogs held Tyrese's arms in the grips of their teeth.

Tyrese struggled against all of them, but he was no match for the big sister protecting her little sister, for the FBI agent who always got his man and for the two German shepherds who would protect their handlers to their deaths.

Parker sat on the ground beside Veronica and wrapped his arm around her shoulders to pull her close. She let her head fall to his shoulder, not wanting to go anywhere. Her teeth chattered, but the peace that cloaked her warmed her whole body.

"It's over," he said with a sound of relief, kissing her temple. She felt a bit of desperation and a whole lot of joy in his touch. She felt the same joy, and suddenly, Christmas fell within her grasp again.

As Theo led the apprehended kidnapper away to his unmarked car, Veronica called out to him, "Merry Christmas, Theo. Give that baby a kiss for us when he or she makes her debut into the world."

"I'm sure Willow will be having you out soon enough," Theo said.

Another car pulled up alongside Theo's. Two National Park Police officers stepped from the vehicle, and she could hear Theo telling them the scene was stable and the threat had been extinguished.

"But there's a few people who could use a place to dry off and warm up," Theo said as he shut his rear door on Tyrese. He got in his vehicle and took off as the officers came around the two remaining cars.

"We heard the gunshots and came to inspect. I'm glad we're not looking at a lot of paperwork before the holidays," one of the men said with a cheeky grin.

The other said, "Why don't you all come back to the lodge and get dried up? We have some clothes you could use and a fire blazing."

Veronica wasn't about to turn down that offer. But first, she had someone to thank. After getting to her feet, she walked toward the shore and met her sister there.

"I'm sorry I kicked you out of my car," Jasmin said, but she didn't really look sorry.

"I'm sure you would do it again if the need arose," Veronica replied.

"Absolutely." Jasmin lifted her face to meet Veronica's gaze, and the two women shared a small smile before reaching for each other and wrapping their arms tightly around one another.

"Don't ever cut me out again," Veronica whispered. "I don't need protecting anymore."

Jasmin nodded. "I believe you've proven that you're tougher than I am."

"Not quite, but definitely a close second."

As Veronica stepped away, she caught sight of Parker standing with the dogs. The support emanating from his eyes filled her heart to overflowing.

"He looks like he's in love," Jasmin whispered beside her.

"Don't be ridiculous," Veronica chided her sister, but what if he was? Veronica pushed away the thought. "We've just been through a lot together. Isn't that enough?"

"It may not be enough for him." Jasmin reached for Veronica's hand and gave it a squeeze. "Take it from me, sister. Good men are hard to find, and Parker Walsh is a good, good man."

As Veronica neared Parker, he captured her gaze and most likely her heart. But she wasn't ready to tell him that. They had been through so much, and he had said he wanted her to keep a clear head. There was nothing clearheaded about professing love for someone after her harrowing experience.

"Shall we go to the lodge?" she asked, suddenly feeling nervous around him.

He bit his lower lip and narrowed his gaze. "I think that's wise. No sense in getting sick after surviving attempted murder."

The three of them and the dogs followed the officers. Jasmin climbed in behind the wheel of her car, and Veronica decided she would go with her sister. She also took Summer as Parker joined the National Park Police with Rosie. Veronica tried not to make it awkward, but with each moment that passed between them, uncertainty set in.

When they reached the lodge, they were handed dry clothes and went their separate ways to vacant rooms. When Veronica emerged from her room, she found Parker by the Christmas tree they had driven by earlier.

The lights glimmered on his face, and when he turned to her, he lifted a hand. "Come here," he said, leaving no room for negotiation.

Veronica stepped forward to stand beside him, but didn't take his hand. She spoke while staring at the Christmas lights on the tree. "I don't want you to feel obligated to hold to anything that was said between us in moments of fear or desperation."

Parker scoffed. "And I want you to hold me to them all. Because I meant every word." His hand remained between them. "I love you, Veronica. I've always loved you. Since the moment I stepped into the PNK9 Unit, you were the woman for me."

"Always?" She stepped a foot closer to him. Her gaze fell on his hand, and she wanted to take it with all her heart.

"And forever," he whispered.

She lifted her gaze to his and let out a deep sigh. Instead of taking his hand, she closed the space between them and moved right into his arms. Her head rested on his shoulder as she embraced the truth of his words.

Lifting her gaze to his, she whispered, "You gave me a second chance when I didn't deserve it. You helped me to forgive myself when I couldn't do it. You loved me when I didn't show you love. You have given me the greatest gift anyone could ever ask for, and all I can say is thank you."

"There is no greater love than unconditional love. How could I withhold it from you when Jesus gave it so freely to me."

"I see that now. And I think this Christmas is going to mean so much more because I do."

Parker smiled widely. She didn't think she'd ever seen so much joy in his eyes. "I'm so happy for you. Your life will never be the same."

"I hope that you will be part of my life, Parker."

His smile flitted from his face as his gaze dropped to her lips. "Are you saying what I think you're saying? Do I dare hope?"

"I'm saying that I love you too. And I will always love you…forever."

His eyes glittered with a sheen of tears. "You have given me the greatest gift I could ever ask for. This Christmas will be the first of many, my love, because I'm never letting you go again."

Veronica reached up and wrapped her arms around his neck. She lifted up on her toes to meet his lips for a kiss filled with enough joy and love to last a lifetime.

When Veronica pulled away, she noticed the dogs sitting up by the fire, their attention locked on the two of them. "We're being watched," Veronica whispered.

Parker glanced over his shoulder to see the K-9s' tilted heads. He looked back at Veronica and found her lips again. "Let them watch. They'll have to get used to it, anyway, because I have big plans for us."

Veronica smiled against his lips. "These plans wouldn't include bells, would they?"

"They sure would. And I don't mean the Christmas kind." Parker pulled his lips from hers. "I want to be your husband. I want to be your partner in life and not just in work. I couldn't imagine anyone else beside me but you, Veronica."

"Oh, Parker, you really are a good, good man, and I would be honored to be your wife and your partner in life."

The tears that had glimmered in his eyes broke free and trailed down his cheeks. He cupped the back of her head and cradled her so lovingly. Veronica felt cherished and protected, but somehow, it didn't make her feel less than adequate. Instead, Parker's love filled her with strength and courage. Parker's love made her whole.

"I'm going to make you proud, Veronica." He cupped her cheek and gave her a sweet kiss.

She held on to his hand and smiled with what she hoped was an expression of her love for him. "You already have."

The two of them held tight, knowing how close they had come to never finding their way back to each other They would never let anything separate them again.

* * * * *

Dear Reader,

I hope you have enjoyed the Pacific Northwest K-9 Unit series this year, as well as Parker and Veronica's story. What a joy it has been to be part of this collection, working closely with all the amazing authors who love to bring you hours of entertainment through their inspiring stories of love and intrigue. I am honored to be a part of the series and honored to bring you this Christmas story.

As beautiful as Christmas stories are, I wanted to reflect on the message of second chances and unconditional love. We all have made mistakes in our lives, but through the power of love and redemption, we can start again. I believe Veronica learned this lesson well, and when it came to forgiving herself, it was Parker that showed her sometimes the hardest person to forgive is yourself. But Parker understood this and made sure Veronica knew that she was completely forgiven. I also believe that Veronica's love was exactly what Parker deserved after his harrowing year of being set up for crimes he didn't commit. In the end, I believe they both received a wonderful Christmas present—their own happily-ever-after.

I love to hear from readers. Please feel free to send me an email at katylee@katyleebooks.com or visit my website at katyleebooks.com.

Peace and joy to you!
Katy Lee

HOLIDAY RESCUE COUNTDOWN

Sharee Stover

For the Sheepdog Peacemakers
who serve to protect us every day.

Blessed are the peacemakers,
for they shall be called the children of God.
—*Matthew* 5:9

ONE

If Dylan Jeong planned to survive the next two weeks with his fifteen-year-old niece, Leah, he'd need to deploy strategic tactics. He'd encountered tough adversaries and skirted political red tape with the best, in his military and law enforcement careers, but she had him digging into the reserves of his counterintelligence training.

With a plastered smile, he faced Leah, prepared to pitch his revised argument, convincing her to help with the Emeryton Christmas parade. "This is the opportunity of a lifetime!" Dylan said, infusing enthusiasm into his tone. "You're a part of the Pacific Northwest K-9 team!"

"Hardly." Leah huffed, attempting to cross her arms over her chest. The candy-cane costume she was wearing hindered her efforts. "If you make me do this, you'll be responsible for my death." She pinned him with a glare that reflected the familiar Jeong-family stubbornness.

Dylan stifled a laugh to keep from agitating her. "There are no reported cases of death by embarrassment."

"Great, mine will be the first." Leah held a firm pout.

"At least you're not alone." Brandie Weller, fellow officer at the PNK9 Unit, joined them in the massive garage staging area. She sported her matching costume. "I'm right there with you." She did an awkward spin.

Leah's pout changed to a frown. "What if someone recognizes me?" She stared at the bright fabric with disdain.

"You live in Chicago," Dylan reminded her. "Doubtful anyone there will see Emeryton, Washington's Christmas parade."

His sister, Tanya, had requested for Leah to stay with him unexpectedly. He'd quickly agreed without pressing for details, aware that Leah's parents were weathering a rocky storm in their marriage. They needed time alone to work through things. He'd do anything necessary to help the family.

"This is your chance to do something wild and brave." Then Brandie whispered, "Besides, we're famous."

Dylan shot her a grateful nod. He had a lot to learn about communicating with a teen girl, and he appreciated Brandie's efforts. "She's right. Our team has celebrated huge wins with our cases."

"Fine." Leah whined the word, but her disposition softened.

"It's perfect parade weather today." Brandie adjusted her headset and mic.

"A great day for a ride." Dylan secured his headset beneath his helmet. The small devices didn't draw attention and allowed them to communicate.

"Do I get one of those?" Leah asked.

"Sorry, no," Dylan said.

Her glare returned.

Ugh.

"Trust me, you don't want one," Brandie added. "The team hears everything you say." She winked, and Leah gave a knowing nod.

Apparently, that was a deterrent. Dylan would take whatever gained Leah's cooperation.

The Saturday parade would kickoff Emeryton's two-week holiday extravaganza which would conclude on New Years Eve.

"The costume hood hides you." Brandie emphasized her comment by pulling the rest of the costume over her head, completing the hook portion of the cane. A white mesh screen hid their faces, while arm holes gave them use of their hands, and the cylindrical base, though narrow, allowed them to walk. Black gloves and shoe covers completed the attire. "We should call this job shadowing." She did a funny side bow.

Leah giggled. "Sure, we're candy cops."

"Exactly," Brandie chuckled.

Relief oozed through Dylan. He'd owe Brandie for helping him with Leah—though he didn't view that as an imposition.

"I'll check in with the rest of the team." Brandie waddled to the float.

Leah's frown returned and Dylan's patience evaporated. "Remember our agreement. No backing out now."

Ridge, his one-hundred-and-fifty-pound Saint Bernard, nudged his hand—always in tune with Dylan's mood. "Even Ridge is dressed for the occasion."

Dylan slid the specially designed protective eye gear—a pair of oversized goggles—over Ridge's head and topped off the look with his black half helmet. Ridge thumped his tail, eager to start their motorcycle ride from his sidecar.

"He's handsome." Leah stroked the dog's head. "Besides the goggles, the sign is my favorite." She gestured at the bright white magnetic sign printed with red and green letters that read *Fleas Navidad* decorating the sidecar.

"Totally Ridge's idea," Dylan teased, earning him a low woof from his search-and-rescue K-9.

"Fine, I'll do it." Leah sighed. "On one condition. Promise you'll take me sightseeing tomorrow?"

"I'm crushed you'd have to ask." Dylan pressed a hand to his chest in a mock gesture of pain. "You know I'm a man of my word."

Leah giggled and rolled her eyes, but her demeanor softened. "Whatever, Uncle Dylan." She swatted at him playfully.

Brandie returned with PNK9 officer Ruby Orton.

"Remind me to schedule myself on vacation next Christmas," Ruby said, carrying bags of miniature candy canes to hand out to the crowd.

"Those are great." Brandie took the proffered treats.

Ruby grinned. "You've got the moves down in that getup."

"It's easy." Brandie twirled.

"Now that's holiday joy, baby sister," Nick Rossi, Ruby's fiancé and the brother Brandie had recently reunited with after almost a lifetime apart, chimed in. He carried his three-year-old daughter, Zoe, who was grinning from ear to ear.

Dylan smiled, relishing the friendship of his PNK9 teammates. Though secretly, he enjoyed Brandie's company most. Not that she had a clue about that, and he intended to keep it that way. In the months they'd worked together, she'd blossomed, especially after they'd solved her own childhood abduction case.

PNK9 had shared in Brandie and Nick's reuniting after nearly two decades of their forced separation. Though her kidnappers had died before they could be charged with her abduction, Brandie's investigative skills, the team's efforts and God's blessing had all helped to reunite the siblings. Brandie hadn't even known Nick was her brother when she'd tried out for a slot with the PNK9 Unit. But her assignment had led her right to Nick, during their investigation of Zoe's—thankfully brief—kidnapping. Those were just two of the many cases they'd solved in the past year. Social media and local-news feel-good stories had contributed to their growing fame, along with Emeryton's request to participate in the parade.

"Can I ride on the motorcycle, Daddy?" Zoe asked.

"Not today. That's Ridge's job," Nick said. "You're gonna help Ruby on the float while I drive it."

Zoe, dressed in a red-and-white jumpsuit

with a candy-cane headband, squealed with delight. Ruby hoisted her to their boss Donovan Fanelli, who was seated beside Pepper, Ruby's black Labrador, Taz, Brandie's recently retired, previous K-9 partner, and Zoe's golden retriever, Goldie.

"Is Chief riding up here, too?" Donovan asked, referencing one of the young bloodhounds the team had rescued in their prior case.

Brandie had chosen Chief, intending to specialize in search and rescue.

"No, he'll walk alongside me. He needs to get used to working with us," Brandie replied, then gestured at the bloodhound. "Come on, Chief."

The dog responded with a yawn and stretch before plodding over to where she waited.

"Ms. Zoe, you're gorgeous!" Brandie pressed both black-gloved hands against her mouth, emphasizing the compliment.

The child beamed. "Auntie Brandie, you look funny."

Brandie did a little dance, eliciting Zoe's giggles. Dylan admired the bond, enjoying the way the youngster brought out Brandie's playful side.

"The crowd's dying to see the K-9s." She removed her hood, then adjusted her mic. "How often do they witness a motorcycle-riding dog?" Brandie slid Chief's leash over her wrist, freeing her hands.

Dylan caught sight of the bloodhound's soulful brown gaze that seemed to say "don't even think about making me ride on that." He chuckled. "No worries, Chief. There's only room for one K-9."

The bloodhound snorted.

"He appreciates that." Brandie tugged up her hood, then helped Leah do the same.

Dylan donned his leather jacket before checking the motorcycle sidecar. He motioned for Ridge to hop in.

Brandie and Dylan were two of the few PNK9 officers who hadn't found love matches this year. Not that he didn't find Brandie attractive. Her raven hair and winning smile had won him over, but they were coworkers, making her off-limits in his book. Dylan couldn't risk losing anyone else he cared about, because his track record had proven that the people he cared for died.

And those events ensured that he would remain a loner.

"Sorry I'm late." PNK9 officer Veronica Eastwood helped her German shepherd, Summer, onto the float, then sat beside her with a grin.

"The gang's all here." Nick started the truck and pulled out of the garage.

Dylan refocused and slid onto the motorcycle. With one last check, he said, "Let's roll."

Brandie and Leah walked alongside the float with Dylan and Ridge trailing. The crisp December air and cobalt sky added to the peaceful morning. Christmas carols played from each display, vying for everyone's attention with competing songs of holiday cheer.

Brandie marveled at the joy emanating from the crowd as they pointed and waved at the PNK9 dogs. Small children sat atop their fathers' shoulders. She imagined the kids were no doubt blissfully counting down the days until they opened their presents under the tree, just as she'd done at their age.

A heaviness hovered over her, making her grateful for the concealing costume. This was the first Christmas she'd spend with her brother, Nick, niece, Zoe, and future sister-in-law, Ruby. Brandie shook her head at the bizarre events from the past year. She'd started with PNK9 bearing the weight of her private search for the truth about herself after finding documents that confirmed the flickers of memories from her abduction. She'd immersed herself in researching cold cases, certain that one explained her life and would satisfy her desire to find her real family. Her biological parents had welcomed Brandie with tears and open arms. They still called her Lizzie— her given name—which she hated. She'd smiled, not wanting to hurt them or appear rude, but she hadn't been Lizzie for a long time.

Brandie wasn't sure who she was. She'd spent so much of her adult life searching for the truth of her past—shoving all those questions without answers into that Lizzie-shaped box and tying it up with a ribbon was impossible.

She should be overjoyed. Her happily-ever-after had arrived.

So why wasn't she?

After two decades of being Brandie Weller, the only child of parents responsible for her childhood abduction, she hadn't finished sorting through her convoluted feelings. There was no handbook to provide the fundamentals of reuniting with one's estranged biological family, or forgiving deceitful abductors. Brandie snorted at her internal sarcasm.

She hadn't found time to deal with it all and hadn't known where to start. Her prayers were complicated these days, but the PNK9 Unit was one thing she continually gave thanks for. Especially Dylan and Ruby. Both were understanding in helping her with the transition. She'd enjoyed getting acquainted with Nick and Zoe too. God had come up with a complex and wonderful plan in uniting them.

A single question left a hiccup in her

faith journey. Why hadn't God protected her from the abduction in the first place?

Leah laughed, tossing candy canes to the crowd, and Chief trotted happily beside her.

She moved to the opposite side of the float and spotted Zoe, who was laughing and clapping on Ruby's lap. Brandie had spent her life sequestered and alone. Suddenly, she was a part of something bigger, which continued to grow with Ruby and Nick's engagement.

The holidays exacerbated the massive emotions. Not that she'd confided her doubts to anyone, especially her teammates.

Not now. She refocused on the event. Chief soaked in the attention, reminding Brandie her hard work had paid off. She was officially a PNK9 officer after a long and difficult try-out period.

And she was currently dressed as a giant candy cane.

"This isn't so bad." Leah sidled up to her.

Brandie glanced at her red-and-white-striped partner, thrilled the teen had joined in the festive spirit. "Does dressing like a giant candy cane qualify as undercover duty?"

Laughter from the team emitted over her earpiece.

"Good one," Ruby said.

Colorful Christmas decorations draped the storefronts. Candy and confetti littered their path. Delicious aromas wafted from vendor carts of roasted almonds and popcorn that were positioned along the route.

The PNK9 group slowed, nearing the halfway point, where the announcer's booth stood opposite the firehouse. The master of ceremonies' voice boomed as he enthusiastically introduced each of the floats and shared sponsor details.

"Here's the Pacific Northwest K-9 team with their giant German shepherd float. Oh, and there are some of the actual K-9s!"

Brandie took the cue and led Chief around for the crowd. He pranced, head lifted high. The bloodhound was made for the spotlight.

Donovan and Ruby descended the float to show off Pepper and Taz along the edge of the trailer, allowing everyone a full view of the K-9s. Goldie sat beside Zoe, who waved and beamed like she owned the place.

A second announcer joined in. "Trailing the float on his motorcycle is PNK9 Officer Dylan Jeong and his search-and-rescue K-9, Ridge."

Cheers rose from the crowd as Dylan revved the engine in response.

A child behind Brandie cooed, "Oh, that dog with the glasses is so cute!"

"Take his picture," declared another onlooker.

Suddenly, the trilling of a familiar Christmas carol grew louder, overriding the throng's applause, the emcee's speaking and other music playing on the accompanying floats.

Where was that racket coming from?

Brandie turned as a rectangular object, about two feet by one foot, wove in and out of the parade traffic in front of them. It appeared to be a mobile Christmas gift traveling on four small tires, like a radio-controlled car. It was wrapped in gold and silver paper and adorned with a massive bow, which must've concealed the speaker, because the music grew louder as it approached.

The crowd clapped, assuming it to be part of the show. Brandie peered through the screen-covered mask and tilted her head. Donovan and Ruby met her confused expression. Dylan lifted the visor of his helmet.

"I don't remember this in the lineup," she said into her mic.

"And what's this special treat?" the first announcer asked.

The object zoomed forward, facing the float and did several spins.

"It's not possible. There's no way," Dylan said in a soft tone. Then, he hollered into the mic, "Nobody panic! Get the crowd to move to the right side of the street immediately."

Like a train wrecking in front of him, Dylan focused on the mobile gift, which was blaring the cheerful Christmas carol and distracting the onlookers from the real danger it posed. People would die if he didn't respond, and fast.

"What's going on?" Brandie asked.

"When the song ends, the box will explode," Dylan said. "It's a bomb."

"Brandie, Leah, get out of there!" Nick exited the driver's seat of the truck. "Use the dogs to divert the crowd."

The group swung into action. Brandie passed her bag of candy to Leah, her voice carrying over Dylan's earpiece. "Take this and let's corral the people for a demonstration."

"I'll tell the announcer," Donovan replied.

"Folks, may I have your attention?" the emcee said. "The PNK9 team will provide an impromptu demo for us! Everyone to the firehouse."

Excited groups hurried to the brick building with Brandie, Nick, Ruby and Leah ushering them inside.

"I'll try to distract it away from you." Dylan revved his engine. As if in response, the present zoomed toward him, spinning in taunting circles around his motorcycle.

And he knew.

The bomb was meant for him.

No! Dylan's past had somehow returned.

How? Impossible! Irving Louter was still incarcerated.

But a Christmas carol spouting from a mobile gift was his signature.

This was how his plan of terror began.

"Yes, sir, head on inside the firehouse," Brandie said to an onlooker.

"Clear the area!" Dylan hollered.

The others had deserted the float, and the eerie trilling of the persistently circling present continued. The giant German shepherd adornment gazed down at him, as though understanding he was helpless to stop what was about to happen.

"Dylan, get out of there!" Donovan ordered.

"I'm going to lead it away," Dylan replied.

"No." Donovan's tone grew more insistent. "Get out of here!"

The present lingered in a menacing dance, stalking Dylan as the song blared.

Dylan drove slowly, allowing the box to stay close.

They'd reached the corner, distanced from

the firehouse, where the spectators were protected behind the doors.

And oblivious to what would happen next.

Over the mic, he heard Brandie and Leah talking.

"What's going on?" Leah asked.

"Just keep everyone inside," Brandie replied.

A child's voice interrupted them. "Daddy, I want to see the motor-go-cycle doggie!"

"Dylan, stop! A boy's chasing after you!" Brandie hollered.

Dylan turned and spotted a preschool-aged boy who'd tugged free from his father's hand and dodged his parent's attempts to catch him. The child bolted for Dylan, catching the attention of the other kids, who also rushed toward the float.

"He's getting to see the dog!"

"Me too! Me too!"

"Get everyone out of here!" Dylan yelled over the headset as the preschooler lunged for Ridge in the sidecar.

Dylan swept the child into his arms and sped away.

The present charged after him as the last notes of the carol blared from the speaker.

Silence.

Then a blast erupted through the night.

TWO

Brandie slid into the seat opposite Dylan. Rescue personnel had finally released everyone from the scene and the remaining PNK9 group had assembled in the renovated bed-and-breakfast sitting room. The remodeled house still maintained its classic decor. Antique cabinets and settees filled the space, and flames crackled from the elaborate fireplace, where stockings hung from the mantel.

Though the facility had closed for the holidays, the owners had kindly donated rooms for the PNK9 Unit, so they'd be close for the parade festivities. The lack of customers provided the needed privacy as they discussed the explosion and prepared for their investigation.

With only a portion of the team available

to work the case, they would have to strategically utilize their assets.

"Maybe I should stick around?" Nick appeared beside her, absorbed in his role of protective brother.

"We'll be fine," Brandie assured him.

With a reluctant nod, Nick helped Zoe into her coat, then gathered Goldie's and Pepper's leashes. He kissed Ruby's cheek, then whispered loud enough for Brandie to hear, "Watch over my sister."

"Always," Ruby replied. "Thanks for taking Pepper home."

"No problem." Nick ushered the Rossi group from the room.

"He worries for you." Ruby squeezed Brandie's hand.

"I know." The feeling was unfamiliar, yet welcome. Brandie shifted on the settee—which was built for looks, not comfort—and contemplated the importance of never letting down her guard. In the short time she'd work with the PNK9 Unit, she'd learned that crime didn't take breaks or holidays. The team had gone from one investigation to another. Once more, she sent up a silent prayer of gratitude that she was a part of the elite group of individuals and K-9s.

"Why this parade?" Ruby passed Brandie a mug filled with warm coffee.

"My question exactly," Donovan said.

Brandie caught a flitting expression that crossed Dylan's face, followed by an almost imperceptible communication between him and Donovan. Brandie spotted deception when others missed it, and she suspected they were withholding information. Why?

"Dylan?" His name escaped her lips before she realized it. Brandie glanced around, wondering if she'd spoken aloud. Based on the curious expressions of her teammates, she had.

He faced her. "Yeah?"

No point avoiding the topic. "What's going on?" Her question came out more accusatory than she'd intended.

Dylan's lack of response confirmed her reservations and contradicted her experience with him. He wasn't a deceitful guy. Was he?

Ruby paced near the fireplace. "Dylan, do you have intel?"

Donovan's cell phone sat on the table, allowing Veronica to participate from her room upstairs. She'd offered to hang out with Leah while the team discussed the information.

Dylan sighed, leaning back in his chair. "It might be nothing."

"Or it might be everything," Ruby retorted.

Dylan stood and walked to the frost-covered window. "I'll need to examine the bomb to confirm my suspicions, but there are similiar aspects from this incident that occurred in prior cases I worked in Seattle." He glanced at Donovan.

Again, an unspoken agreement seemed to pass between the men. What did they know that they didn't want to include and inform the rest of the team? Brandie studied her colleague. Though he upheld a polished exterior—not a single hair was out of place, and there wasn't a wrinkle in his clothes—his lighthearted manner had waned since the bombing. He gave the impression of a man defeated, with his shoulders slumped and shadows lingering on his handsome face. For the first time since she'd started working with PNK9, she observed a chink in his impeccable armor, revealing weakness and uncertainty.

He glanced at Donovan as if asking permission to continue.

"I think it's imperative you give them the facts of the case," Donovan said.

Brandie figured he'd also given an unspoken command to withhold something.

Or was she imagining things? Her natural skeptical nature tainted her perception. Why wouldn't their boss and teammate want them to have the information needed to takedown the bomber?

"I'm all for suspense, but this is ridiculous," Ruby said.

Brandie's instincts flared. Though she'd classify her time with PNK9 Unit as positive, she never fully trusted anyone. After all, she'd spent two decades loving "parents" responsible for her abduction and captivity.

"Five years ago, I worked a serial bomber case in Seattle. His signature included sending a mobile gift into a well-attended parade crowd." Dylan's comment redirected everyone's attention to him. He crossed his arms. "He used Christmas carols, set in a specific order, with the intent of inflicting as much damage as possible. He had four horrific attacks with multiple casualties before my partner and I finally identified him as Irving Louter."

"I remember that name," Veronica said.

"We withheld details regarding the bomb's assembly to prevent instigating a copycat." Dylan fidgeted with a stocking on the mantel. "Only those directly involved— namely, my partner, our commander and I—had the particulars. We narrowed our suspects to Louter after an intense investigation. Evidence tied him to the bombings. He was charged and sentenced to life in prison."

"Is it possible they released him on parole?" Veronica asked over the speakerphone.

"No way." Though Dylan's tone contained authority, uncertainty clung to his fallen expression.

"Veronica, are you comfortable assisting

with the technical aspects of the case while Jasmin is on medical leave? She needs time to rest and recouperate." Donovan referenced the team's most recent investigation involving Jasmin's kidnapping and rescue.

"I'm ahead of you," Veronica replied. "Jasmin's already offered to walk me through anything if I get stuck."

"Excellent. Please verify Louter's still incarcerated," Donovan interjected.

"It's doubtful," Dylan said. "He's not eligible for parole yet."

"I'll see what I can find, however, since it's a weekend, we might have to wait until Monday when the office staff returns to answer the main line," Veronica responded.

"So we're thinking a copycat?" Ruby asked.

"That's my assumption. He'll stay consistent with Louter's signature." Dylan paced a small area near the window, glancing out occasionally. "We can't bank on that as his sole MO."

"It's a starting point," Donovan said.

Dylan walked to where the dogs had assembled in the space farthest from the fireplace. "If the perpetrator's pattern holds true, there will be several bombings before the end of the year."

Ruby pinned Dylan with an inquisitive stare. "How many?"

"Four, at least, by New Year's Eve."

"We have to stop him before he sets them," Ruby added, stating the obvious.

"How?" Brandie asked.

"By dissecting Christmas-carol lyrics," Dylan said. "He'll pinpoint words revealing the bomb locations."

"That's twisted," Veronica said. "He uses the same carols and order?"

"Yes, but he chooses different key words." Dylan frowned. "The media released the list of songs during the investigation, making them public knowledge. That also provides a roadmap for a copycat."

"But if he mixes them up…" Ruby began.

"We won't know until the second bombing." Dylan winced. "I'll scan my notes and compile a reference list."

"Does the bomber use specific words as in every noun or places in the song?" Brandie asked.

Dylan shook his head. "Nope. That's the strange part." He stood taller, his shoulders back. "We'll decipher his plan because Louter wants us to."

"Who's the intended target?" Ruby asked.

He sighed. "Me."

"I don't understand," Donovan inserted.

"Elaborate, please," Brandie said.

"Louter hates me, and he lives for the chase. He likes teasing cops with a twisted game of cat and mouse. It's part of the thrill. Thus, he'll lead us to the bombs." Dylan dropped onto the chair again. "I put him away, and he promised revenge five years ago. If this is a copycat, he's probably an extension for Louter, therefore, he's targeting me. But he'll ensure maximum destruction in the process."

Brandie sucked in a breath. The bomber would hurt anyone close to Dylan too. "Leah."

Dylan met her gaze, sadness lingering in his eyes. "She needs protective custody at my house in Ashford until we apprehend him."

"Ruby and I will take shifts with her there," Veronica said.

"Absolutely." Ruby nodded emphatically. "We'll help y'all any way possible and keep Leah safe." Ruby's southern accent occasionally reappeared when she spoke.

"Thanks, guys." For the first time since the bombing, relief softened Dylan's features. "I can't work while worrying about her."

"We get that." Compassion welled within Brandie.

Her reunion with Nick had revealed the kindness of brotherly concern. Prior to that, she'd only experienced obsessive isolation. Brandie chastised herself for her previous thoughts, concluding that Dylan's change of demeanor was simply worry for his niece.

"I'll take the remaining dogs to the kennels at HQ while we work." Donovan gestured toward the sleeping K-9s. "They're great SAR experts, but none of them is trained in explosion detection."

At Donovan's declaration, Chief sat up, crossing his front paws in a regal position.

The bloodhound lifted his head, and his droopy eyes and ears perked slightly.

"I'll take Ridge home," Dylan said.

Their commander's assessment was correct, and though Brandie hated to be away from the dogs, they needed an expert. "We need Star." She referred to PNK9 member Willow Bates's German shorthaired pointer. "Willow is in her last pregnancy trimester."

"Due any day," Ruby added.

"She can't help us in the case, and Theo needs to be with her," Veronica replied, reminding them of Willow's husband and fellow teammate.

"Star is trained to work with other handlers," Donovan explained.

Brandie hesitated, the idea sprouting. Would Donovan think her too forward if she asked to be Star's handler?

He faced her, as though in response to her unspoken thoughts. "Let's request Willow loan Star to Brandie."

"I'll pick her up," Brandie blurted. Her ears warmed at the outburst. She lifted her chin defiantly. At least she was brave enough to offer. That wouldn't have happened six months ago, but her time with the PNK9 group had built her confidence as a handler.

"Thanks, Brandie," Donovan said.

She beamed at his approval.

"Sounds good." Ruby stood.

Brandie marveled at the team's supportive attitude. None vied with the other for position.

"Dylan, get us the carol list," Donovan added. "We need the bomber's next target. I'll contact Willow and advise Brandie's on the way."

"Roger that," Dylan replied.

"I'll have the local bomb squad check your house before you return there," Donovan continued. "Veronica and Ruby travel with Dylan and get Leah situated at the house. Decide between yourselves on a shift schedule then one of you reconvene here in person, the other via telephone ASAP."

"Roger that." Veronica clicked off.

"Willow will have Star ready to go." Donovan addressed Brandie as she donned her coat and gloves. "Do you have the info?"

"I have her address in my contacts." Brandie wouldn't admit her apprehension at driving the two-and-a-half-hour commute alone. She was a real full-time member of the PNK9 group and the last thing she wanted was them second-guessing her capabilities. Particularly the simple assignment of picking up a dog. The mild winter weather meant clear and dry roads. "I'll keep you updated."

Donovan nodded. "We won't allow this criminal to get away with ruining Emeryton's holiday events. Especially at the cost of innocent lives."

"We'll get him." Dylan met Brandie's gaze then averted his eyes.

His soft response incited her nosiness. Had he spoken the words for their benefit, or his?

After all the PNK9 team had encountered, she had no doubt they'd takedown the bomber. She just prayed they did so before he struck again.

Dylan exited the room without another word, and Ruby met her confused look. Curiosity had Brandie determined to explain

Dylan's uncharacteristic standoffishness. Instinct said there was more to the bomber story than he'd shared, and she intended to find out what.

Dylan flicked a glance in the rearview mirror, where Ruby's SUV followed him. Veronica rode with her and they traveled the curvy roads leading to his secluded house. He hated keeping information from his teammates, but conveying those particulars would overwhelm him.

How had Louter or a possible copycat working for him found Dylan? Why now?

Dylan's home wasn't listed in his name, therefore, tax records wouldn't lead the bomber there. Once he'd provided that small detail to the team, thankfully, no one had asked him to elaborate.

After much private discussion, Donovan had acquiesced to Dylan's request to withhold the details of Louter murdering Dylan's Seattle partners. Their deaths weren't relevant to the current investigation, and he refused to deal with the accompanying pain. He had to focus on stopping the next bomb.

"How long are Ruby and Veronica staying with me?" Leah whined from the passenger seat. "I'm not a baby. I don't need a sitter."

"It's not like that. They'll take turns hanging out with you once we get you settled." Impatience wove through Dylan, and he reminded himself that his niece lived a privileged life for the most part. She certainly didn't experience bombers, killers or drug runners daily. This was scary for her, and she was oblivious as to how far the bomber would go. If, in fact, it was a copycat, which it had to be, would he target anyone around Dylan? Would Louter's crony go after the rest of PNK9 too?

Brandie's face emerged in his mind first. He couldn't bear another loss. Not like Michelle.

Leah continued grousing, and Dylan didn't correct or chastise her. Better for her to think he had to work than to tell her the truth. Scaring and upsetting his niece benefited no one. He'd take her pouting and anger at him over terrorizing the poor teen.

If the copycat stayed true to Louter's form, he'd do whatever it took to ensure he met his goal.

Ridge shifted in the back seat.

"You'll have Ridge to keep you company too," Dylan said. At least for tonight. The dog needed a little rest after the bombing chaos.

That gave her pause. At the mention of his name, the Saint Bernard leaned in and rested his mammoth head on the console.

"Hi, Ridge," Leah grumbled.

The K-9 licked her cheek, eliciting a giggle from the teen. "Ew." She swiped away the moisture and stroked the dog's fur.

Relieved the animal had provided a moment of reprieve from Leah's tantrum, Dylan smiled. "Dude, no unsolicited kisses." The gentle chastisement also earned Dylan a massive lick on the side of his face. "*Ew* is right," he chuckled. "Back to your seat, Ridge."

The Saint Bernard harrumphed and withdrew to his spot.

"He hates being left out of discussions," Dylan explained.

"Relatable," Leah griped. "This is ridiculous. You promised to take me sightseeing!"

"We will. But I must work today."

"It's almost Christmas and we'll miss all the town events!"

"I know."

"So instead of doing anything fun, I'm a hostage at your house." Leah crossed her arms over her chest, a firm pout planted on her lips.

Lord, give me wisdom and patience. Dylan gripped the steering wheel tighter. "Hopefully, this won't take long." An empty promise, but he struggled to find comforting words.

"Are you sure it was a bomb?" Leah twisted in the seat, facing him. "Maybe it was just a fireworks-rigged thing. I mean why would anyone hurt people during a parade?"

Dylan's throat tightened. He hated deception of any kind. How did he tell his sheltered, fifteen-year-old niece that a crazed serial bomber sought revenge on him? She didn't need to bear the weight of knowing Louter had killed Dylan's Seattle PD partners—who'd also been his closest friends—during the takedown and planned to do the same to Dylan.

Though he fought the memories, images of Michelle King and his German shepherd K-9, Pete, battled for his attention.

The dream team. That's what everyone called the three of them. He and Michelle had melded together. Never in a romantic way. In fact, her engagement to his best friend from the military, Flynn, had made them more like family. And then Dylan had cost Michelle's and K-9 Pete's lives.

He'd vowed to never get involved with his coworkers beyond the duties of the job. And he'd failed. PNK9 was family to him too. And over the past few months, he and Brandie had grown closer.

"Uncle Dylan?" Leah persisted. "You're ignoring me."

"I'm not." He swallowed the lump stuck in this throat.

"Can't you stay with me until you're sure the team needs you?"

His heart wrenched at the plea in her voice. "I'm the one with the info, kiddo. We must investigate what happened today. Rest assured PNK9 is the best."

"Whatever," Leah grunted.

The remainder of the drive, Dylan did his best to engage Leah in conversation, but she met his questions with pathetic responses of *yes, no* and *I don't know.*

He turned from the major highway onto the road that narrowed into a single lane, winding through the forested landscape, nearing his property. By the time he reached his house, he was mentally and physically exhausted. He exhaled relief at his modest ranch-style home that sat nestled inside an abundance of lush evergreens. A tall chain-link fence separated his land, and a smattering of trees filled the area amid bushes and other greenery. None of which he'd planted. Having a green thumb wasn't his forte, but he'd benefited from the previous owners, who'd taken time to elegantly landscape the grounds.

Grateful Donovan had arranged for local bomb techs to inspect his house prior to their return, Dylan parked on the side, motioning for Veronica to take the space in the attached two-car garage.

"Why can't I stay with you?" Leah whined, sounding like a child.

Dylan faced her, his patience evaporating, and prepared to unleash his father's strict disciplinarian style. At the sight of his niece, words failed him. He was struck by how much she resembled his baby sister, Tanya. Leah's black-as-night, long hair and soft brown eyes—sans makeup—revealed her natural beauty. She studied him, the way she had as a little girl, and it melted his heart.

Was he making a mistake, leaving Leah here? Should she stay with him?

No. Her safety required distance from the investigation. Ashford was more than an hour from Emeryton. With Veronica and Ruby taking shifts to watch her, Leah was in the best possible hands.

"I promise as soon as this is done, we'll do all the sightseeing and shopping you want," Dylan assured her. "In fact, you might want to create a list of things you're interested in. I'm sure Ruby and Veronica will offer suggestions. They're great resources on places to visit."

At the prospect of shopping, Leah perked up. She maintained a hint of the whine in her tone as she said, "Fine."

Dylan smiled. "Thanks, Leah."

She shrugged and pushed open the door, but he didn't miss her small grin. He'd take the mini win.

Dylan released Ridge, who bounded toward the tree line.

"Are you sure he won't run away?" Concern hovered in Leah's peaked eyebrows.

"Nope. These are his stomping grounds. He's determined to deal with the impetuous squirrel who takes a personal interest in tormenting him. Ridge ensures the rodent knows his place whenever we return."

Leah giggled, a sweet sound, warming Dylan's heart.

Veronica and Ruby exited the SUV just as Nick pulled up and parked beside Dylan's vehicle. "I brought food for the women." He exited the truck, holding bags in explanation.

"You think of everything." Ruby helped Zoe out and they carried the groceries inside.

Dylan appreciated their support since his cupboards weren't stocked for hosting company. He'd planned to take Leah out to eat before the bombing. "Thank you." He exchanged a fist-bump with Nick.

"No problem. Zoe wanted to visit Leah."

They joined the women in the house. Veronica placed her laptop on the table. Leah headed to the guest room in the back of the home.

Zoe skipped after her. "Leah, wait for me."

Though Leah appeared annoyed, a twinkle in her eye said she'd taken to the little girl. "Well come on, then."

Nick laughed. "Those two are doing fine together."

"Zoe's good for Leah." Dylan lowered his voice. "She needs the reminder that the world does not spin on a Leah axis."

"Keep thinking that." Nick chuckled. "I assure you, the deflection is temporary."

Ruby swatted playfully at him. "You

might want to rethink that statement, Nick Rossi." He swept her into his arms and kissed her full on the lips. "My humblest apologies."

Ruby laughed, shoving him away. "Men."

"You two are *so* cute." Veronica rolled her eyes.

"Yeah, knock it off," Dylan teased.

The PNK9 group was his family, and he wouldn't allow anyone to hurt them. He couldn't bear to lose them.

They had to stop the bomber before he struck again.

THREE

The drive to Willow's Port Angeles house provided time for Brandie to overthink the case, Dylan and herself. Light snow feathered her windshield with smatterings of white flakes, enough to blanket the road but not worth turning on the wipers. Like her surroundings, Brandie's thoughts fluttered in a hazy layer in her mind.

She couldn't shake the feeling Dylan was hiding something pertaining to the case. What motive would he have, though? If Brandie had learned anything, it was trust no one completely. Still, she detested doubting her teammate.

She snorted. Who was she kidding?

A lifetime of deception by her abductors had given her a serious suspicion of everyone. As exhausting as it was to live that way, it came naturally to her.

The past months with PNK9 had helped her to work through some of her issues, and reuniting with Nick and her biological parents was a dream come true. But those old needles remained stuck in her heart, and she couldn't shake them. Dishonesty or deception ignited her insecurities like a torch.

Dylan not trusting her with information hurt most. She'd enjoyed his company in the cases they'd worked together. And his standoffishness was a huge step backward in their work relationship.

Brandie paused, pondering the word. No, that wasn't all they had. They'd become friends.

Think the best rather than assume the worst, Donovan had told her repeatedly.

"I want to," Brandie said aloud. "Lord, how do I do that when I'm compelled to protect myself?"

No audible answer provided wisdom, and she tumbled back into her thoughts.

Brandie merged onto the toll road, which

she'd normally avoid, but it was the fastest route to Port Angeles.

She turned up the radio, drowning her contemplations in music. The road curved around a bend, and she lightly pressed the brakes.

The car didn't slow.

Not wanting to skid on the slick ground, she again tapped the pedal.

A snap and her foot slammed the floorboard.

Brandie gasped, gripping the steering wheel.

Instinctively, she continued pumping the failing brakes while her car gained speed. Panic sucked the breath from her lungs.

The downhill slope increased her rapid descent. Brandie clung to the wheel, navigating the twisted path as the vehicle skidded around the corners.

"Lord, help me!" Brandie squealed as the road veered right.

The passenger side slid dangerously close to the guardrail and scraped it, filling the sedan with the sickening sound of metal-on-metal.

She cranked the wheel, coasting to the left.

Heart pounding through her chest, she offered a prayer of gratitude for the barrier and tried to remember the correct procedure for the situation.

Neutral.

Brandie shifted gears and the automatic transmission growled its disapproval. Her speed decreased, and a line of evergreens loomed ahead.

She careened toward the massive greenery, and Brandie tugged the wheel.

It spun without effecting the direction of the vehicle.

The car refused to cooperate.

What was happening?

She sped forward, out of control and straight for the evergreens.

Brandie braced for impact.

A slam halted the vehicle and she stared at the trunk of the immense tree, kissing the hood of her car. Brandie quickly shut off the engine and leaned her forehead against the steering wheel, gasping.

What had just happened? She reached for her phone and called Donovan.

"Brandie, what's wrong?"

His voice offered hope, like a beacon, and her throat tightened with emotion. "My. C-c-car," she stuttered, then tried again. "I have no brakes or steering."

"Are you okay?"

"Y-y-y-yes," she stammered as the adrenaline dump consumed her body.

"I'll track you via your cell phone. I'm on my way and will request rescue and a tow truck for you."

"Th-thank you." Brandie's teeth chattered so hard they hurt.

"Stay put." Donovan disconnected.

Had the situation not terrified her to her core, Brandie would've laughed at the comment. What else could she do?

She called Willow next and updated her.

"Oh, no! Are you all right?" Willow asked. "Do you want me to send Theo?"

"I'm fine," Brandie assured her teammate, mentally berating herself for upsetting the pregnant woman. She infused a calmness she didn't feel into her voice. "Donovan's got it under control. However, we'll be delayed picking up Star."

"Are you sure?"

Willow didn't buy it. Why should she? Brandie's teeth still chattered uncontrollably.

"Really. It's fine."

"We're ready whenever you get here. Be careful."

"Will do." Brandie disconnected and leaned back against the headrest as tears threatened.

She blinked them away, focusing on the windshield covered in the fluffy white flakes.

Auto repair wasn't in her repertoire, however, putting up the hood and activating the hazard lights would warn passersby of her distress. She reached for the release and pressed the large triangular button, then pushed open the door. Not an easy task, considering the heavy evergreen branches hugged her car on both sides.

She inched her way from the vehicle and glanced out at the road, grateful it wasn't nighttime.

Except for her car wedged between two colossal trees, the surrounding scenery was picturesque. Once more, she appreciated the branches that had hindered the crash from fully impacting the tree trunk.

Brandie walked to the front of the vehicle and lifted the hood, securing it upright with the small rod. Sirens wailed in the distance, then grew closer, and she exhaled relief.

Red and blue strobing lights rounded the bend, announcing rescue had arrived.

A mammoth fire truck and ambulance pulled in behind her. The crews placed flares to warn any oncoming drivers of the accident.

Brandie approached the two medics exiting the rig. "Ma'am, is that your vehicle?" The driver gestured at the car.

She stifled a grin. As if there were other vehicles stuck in the tree. "Yes, there was some kind of mechanical failure."

"Looks like you did a great job of navigating away from the edge," the second medic said.

"Believe me, it was more happenstance than my skilled driving."

"Is there anyone else in the car?" the first medic asked.

"No, just me."

"Let's check you out." The second waved her to follow him.

"Really, I'm fine," Brandie assured them, though her teeth continued to chatter from the cold. Even with her goose-down parka, gloves and a stocking cap, the adrenaline did a number on her.

"Protocol," the first replied. "Let's move to the rig for privacy from the chaos."

Arguing was useless, and she was stuck waiting for Donovan, anyway. Brandie complied, trailing the medics to the opened rear ambulance doors. She sat on the edge. The second medic climbed inside and returned with a blanket that he draped over her shoulders. She gratefully snuggled into the warmth while answering the first medic's questions.

After checking her vitals, Brandie reassured them she was fine, so they stopped hovering.

Donovan's familiar SUV approached, and Brandie exhaled relief. "That's my boss," she explained, hopping down from the rig.

Donovan parked to the side, ensuring he'd

not blocked the rescue personnel, and slid out of the driver's seat. "Brandie, are you okay?" His breath clouded from the cold.

Tears threatened at his concern for her. Donovan was the chief of the PNK9 Unit, but he never used his position of power against them. He truly cared.

She blinked away the tears. Though her smile shook on her lips, she refused to give in to the emotion. "I'm fine."

Donovan's creased forehead said he didn't believe her, but he didn't press. She'd lose her composure if he did.

"They've got things handled. Let me talk to the rescue personnel. I've already got a tow truck in process. They'll transfer your vehicle to Emeryton for repair." He gestured at his SUV. "Unless you need something from the car, climb into the SUV and get warmed up."

"Just my purse," Brandie said.

"I'll grab that for you."

She nodded and headed for his vehicle. Though she'd made an effort to ensure everyone she was nonplussed by the events,

Brandie's mind hovered around the big question.

Was the car's failure coincidental, or was the bomber responsible?

Donovan and Brandie had picked up Star, but the incident had delayed the team's investigation until the following morning.

Dylan's emotions ran high. "He could've killed her!"

"But he didn't." Donovan stood in the bed and breakfast's parlor, leaning against the closed door. "We aren't certain it's the copycat bomber. Don't jump to conclusions. Let's work the clues."

"It wasn't a coincidence." Dylan faced his boss and friend. "He's coming for me."

Only Donovan was aware of the full extent of his past. It was a secret he'd promised to keep unless it became necessary to share the details with the team.

"I agree, the attack is conveniently timed, but Brandie wasn't driving a PNK9 vehicle. How would he gain intel on her personal car?"

Dylan disagreed, but he couldn't refute

the information with facts. Somehow, the copycat had discovered Brandie's connection to Dylan, and he'd sought to hurt her. The incident reinforced his mission to get her as far away from the danger as possible. "I don't want anyone else to get hurt."

"Then let's do what PNK9 does best," Donovan said, crossing the room. "We'll get him."

Dylan nodded mutely and trailed his boss to where Ruby and Brandie sat waiting. Veronica opted to stay with Leah at Dylan's house which permitted her to continue working the technical aspects and participate via cell phone.

He avoided their curious gazes, especially Brandie's. Dylan did his best to move away from her and stand at the opposite end of the space. Images from what Donovan explained had happened in her accident flooded him, swarming Dylan with guilt and fear. *She's okay.* He'd repeated the words to remind himself of that fact. Cling to the truth, not the fear of things that didn't happen.

Except the next time she might not be,

and he'd not take that risk. He had to convince her to go with Nick. Dylan wanted as much distance between him and the ones he cared about as possible. If he reminded her that as an officer, she would be able to protect her brother and niece, should the copycat dare to go after them, Brandie might take him up on the suggestion.

Ruby listened to Brandie as she recounted the accident. The cell phone on the table showed Veronica's contact info.

"Guys, I'm telling you, I know how this guy thinks," Dylan blurted, gaining their attention. The discussion stopped, and he continued. "Or, at least how Louter thinks. He'll target each of you." He met Brandie's wide eyes and averted his gaze.

"We're not backing down," Ruby said.

"Agreed. Pretending he won't get to us is counterproductive," Dylan replied.

"So what do you suggest?" Veronica asked.

Dylan inhaled. "Brandie, Leah really likes you. Maybe you and Nick should move her to his house? Provide protective detail for her there."

Brandie frowned. "She's a sweet girl, Dylan. However, between Ruby and Veronica alternating shifts, they've got it covered." She quirked an eyebrow at him, indicating she wasn't buying his suggestion.

"I must side with Brandie," Donovan said. "Nick has Zoe to consider, as well. It behooves Leah for Veronica and Ruby to alternate staying with her," Donovan said. "Brandie's skills are best utilized here."

"Louter, or whoever is doing this, has already proven he'll go after the team." Dylan fisted his hands at his side. They did not understand. And he didn't elaborate by explaining the copycat would focus on the ones he cared most about. That description fit Brandie. Even if he'd never told her.

"Which means none of us is out of his sights," Brandie replied, jaw tight. She lifted her chin in defiance. "I'm not leaving this investigation."

"Leah is safe with Ruby and I trading off shifts," Veronica insisted. "It also allows me to keep tabs on Jasmin via video messaging as she heals." Veronica referenced her sister, the unit's technical expert, and the kidnapping ordeal she'd encountered at the hands of her ex-husband.

"How's she doing?" Brandie asked.

"Much better," Veronica replied.

Dylan wanted to scream, but he was losing the argument and the frown on Donovan's face warned him to discontinue the debate.

"Brandie and Willow have coordinated the skills for using Star to begin the detection work," Ruby said.

They were ganging up on him. Dylan restrained his groan. "Louter's copycat will stay to his MO and start by going after the women on the team." Just like he had with Michelle.

"So we're supposed to go into hiding?" Brandie snorted. "Not happening."

"Dylan, we're all aware of the risks we take every day," Ruby replied.

"The faster we work the clues, find this guy and stop him, the faster we'll be able to put this mess behind us," Veronica inserted.

Dylan raised his hands in surrender,

though his mind contended they were wrong. "Fine."

"Now that we've discussed that to death, let's focus on our next steps," Donovan said, reclaiming his phone.

The group moved to the dining table, where they sat as Dylan passed out printed Christmas-carol lyrics. "Here's the list of songs in the order the bomber will use. He will focus on key words within the lyrics." He dropped onto the chair opposite Brandie. "If he stays consistent with Louter's pattern, he'll go to this one for his next bomb."

Each member quietly studied the paper.

"The word *halls* stands out to me," Brandie said. "That could reference a lot of places, like an event center."

Dylan nodded. "Or a theater."

"What about city hall?" Ruby asked.

"All valid options," Donovan said, "Veronica, please send us a list of buildings in Emeryton that fit that category."

"Already on it," she replied.

Within seconds, their phones chimed with maps.

"I can't say this emphatically enough," Dylan began. "If Louter has trained this guy, or if he's studied Louter for any length of time, he'll use the same tactics. Louter loved to play a cat-and-mouse kind of game with the victims. He wants to lure them because he thrills in getting the most out of his efforts." He winced. "Mass casualties are his favorite, but there's always one major target. He will normally leave that person until the very end. He doesn't mind them getting hurt, but he won't kill the intended target until he's finished toying with law enforcement." The way he'd targeted Michelle, luring her to her death. Dylan swallowed hard. "Until we know otherwise, assume that's me."

"But if what you're saying is true, why go after you directly at the parade?" Ruby asked. "Wouldn't he focus on the crowd or us?"

"He did." Dylan thought back to the moment when the bomb had swerved toward the children, and he'd intercepted.

"He was present at the parade, within the

crowd or possibly watching from one of the buildings," Veronica stated.

"Definitely," Dylan said. "He maneuvers the bomb using a remote control, allowing him to watch the results of his destruction."

"I'll look at footage from the storefront security cameras," Veronica offered. "If I need help, I'm sure Jasmin can walk me through it."

"Only if she feels up to it," Donovan replied.

"She claims she's bored," Veronica chuckled. "Parker's keeping her company and making sure she doesn't leave her house. Which is code for preventing her from doing anything outside of doctor's orders." Parker was also a PNK9 officer—and Veronica's fiancé.

"Excellent," Donovan said.

"Please don't take this the wrong way—I don't mean to sound arrogant, but explosives used to be my specialty," Dylan inserted, redirecting the discussion.

"His military career included explosive training and disarmament," Donovan explained.

Dylan shot him a glare and shook his head, but the damage was done. The comment would lead to other questions and gratitude for his service that he didn't deserve. They had no idea they were working with a pathetic failure.

"If you have questions, ask him," Donovan continued. "Don't be a hero."

"Let's use the Emeryton map and section out areas for our assignments," Brandie suggested.

"Veronica, if you don't mind taking a longer shift with Leah, I'll stay here and take the north and east side of town," Ruby added.

"No problem," Veronica said.

Brandie nodded. "Dylan and I can tackle the west and south."

"I'll contact the local police department and see if they'll let us view the bomb," Donovan replied. "Okay, team, let's divide and conquer." He got to his feet, initiating the rest of the group to do the same.

They exited the dining area, walking to their respective rooms to grab their coats and gloves. Dylan reached for Brandie as she approached him at the door. She spun on her heel, irritation flickering in her dark eyes as she faced him. He inhaled a fortifying breath and said, "We could do some of this virtually. Brandie, you should stay with Nick and work on deciphering more of the clues."

"Knock it off, Dylan." She swatted away his hand. "I'm as capable as everyone else here of working this case."

"You are, but—" Words eluded him.

"But? Who do you think you are?"

Taken aback by her outburst, Dylan's mouth hung open. She'd never snapped at him that way before. Clearly, he'd overstepped his boundaries with her. He attempted to salvage the discussion. "I didn't mean—"

"Worry about yourself. I'm a skilled handler. I earned my position on this team and have worked the same cases you have."

"Yes, it's just—"

"Just what? Stop pushing me to hang out with Nick. Is Donovan telling you to propel our family relationship? Or is Ruby?

I'm tired of everyone thinking Nick and I need to be connected at the hip."

"No. Not at all." Dylan blinked, confused by her tirade. He'd never considered how the team's involvement with the recently reunited siblings might be a bad thing. "I'm sorry. I shouldn't have said anything."

"No, you shouldn't." Her response was harsh, but her demeanor softened.

"I'll grab my things and meet you and Star here?" If he couldn't keep her from the action, he'd protect her by staying by her side. Whatever it took.

She sighed. "Great idea."

At the mention of her name, the German shorthaired pointer moved to Brandie's side.

"I'd say she's ready to work." Dylan smiled and stroked the dog's velvety ears.

Donovan returned. "Just got off the phone with the Emeryton PD and they've authorized you and Brandie to view the bomb. You can't take anything, but get as many pictures as possible to share with the team."

"Roger that," Dylan said. "Let's do this."

He exited the room before he did anything else stupid to upset Brandie.

Time to work on a new strategy.

FOUR

Brandie and Dylan paced the Emeryton police department foyer, waiting for the officer to escort them to the bomb's holding room. The agency policy prevented them from taking Star in with them, so they'd had to leave her in the police canine kennel until they'd finished.

At last, a lanky man dressed in a brown uniform and silver badge approached wearing a somber expression. "Follow me."

Brandie took the lead and Dylan didn't argue. Probably in response to her biting his head off at the bed-and-breakfast. They trailed the officer to the furthest end of the hall. He swiped an identification badge and the lock clicked. "Don't touch anything." He pushed open the door.

Brandie did her best not to roll her eyes at

his unnecessary comment as she and Dylan entered. "Thank you."

A thud confirmed the door had closed. Her gaze remained focused on the soft light, glowing above an object positioned on a table at the far side of the rectangular room. She walked toward the display.

A single set of footsteps echoed in the windowless space behind her. Brandie glanced over her shoulder and paused. Dylan stood beside her, but the officer remained near the door.

Of course—he wouldn't leave them alone here.

She turned and continued forward. The remnants of the bomb were spread on the table. The colorful snowman wrapping paper was singed from the fire, exposing the device's innards. An intricate braid of detonation wires were twisted inside, though most of it had melted together. The short pieces that were intact revealed a distinct pattern like nothing she'd seen before.

"Is it okay if we take pictures for our team?" Brandie asked as a professional courtesy.

"Yes." The officer crossed his arms, as he scrutinized their every move.

Dylan used his cell phone to capture images of the bomb from different angles. The time he spent focusing on the wires told her volumes about the destructive device sitting before them. He didn't speak throughout the process, and she remained quiet.

He pocketed his phone and said, "I think that's all we need unless you have questions?"

Brandie shook her head. "No." At least none she'd ask with the officer watching them.

Dylan led the way out. "Thank you for your time."

The officer gave a single nod as they exited the room.

They retrieved Star from the PD kennels and headed outside.

Brandie could hold her tongue no longer. "Well?"

Dylan didn't answer until they'd slid into the SUV. "It's him or at least his protégé."

"You're certain?"

"Yes, we never released his signature

four-strand braid or the wire colors to the public." He gripped the steering wheel.

"Time to dive into my specialty." Brandie snapped her seat belt.

Dylan glanced at her. "And that is?"

"Research."

"Ah, yes." He chuckled and started the SUV. "Let's check out the map locations Veronica sent. We want to maximize the short remaining daylight hours."

Emeryton was a small town, so it wouldn't take them long. Dylan drove to city hall, tackling the building with the *hall* lyrics that was closest to the police department on their route.

Brandie leashed Star and they made their way around the perimeter, allowing the K-9 to lead. The old two-story, brick-and-stone building sat deserted for the holidays, except for the security guard who met them at the front door. Donovan had already called ahead and they'd been granted clearance, expediting the search.

"I'll lock the door behind you as the facility is closed." No inflection in his tone.

Brandie guessed the man to be in his fifties or sixties, based on his weathered skin and white hair peeking from beneath his uniform hat. She caught a glimpse of his nameplate. *J. Smith.* "I'm Brandie Weller. This is my partner, Dylan Jeong."

Dylan extended his hand and Smith reciprocated without reply. Instead, he focused on Star standing beside Brandie. The security guard smiled, his eyes sparkling. "Who's this?" He kneeled and glanced up. "Oops. May I pet her?"

"Of course." Brandie chuckled. "This is Star."

At the mention of her name, the K-9 sat pretty.

"Aren't you a lovely lady," the man cooed.

Dogs had a way of easing uncomfortable situations, which never surprised Brandie.

"It's a slow day," Smith said. "I'll escort you."

Amusement hovered in Dylan's grin. "Sounds like a plan. We let Star lead since she has the power sniffer."

"Absolutely." Smith shifted, allowing Brandie and Star to move ahead of him.

"Star, search."

Their footsteps echoed in an eerie rhythm on the marble floor. Star sniffed a path along the first level without indicating. They made their way to the second level, Smith keeping in stride with them. After a thorough quest and no indications, they returned to the foyer.

"Thank you," Brandie said.

"I hope you find what you're looking for." Smith smiled.

If only he knew. Clearly, Donovan hadn't shared all the reasons for their arrival.

Brandie and Dylan went to the college next, working through all the buildings with *hall* in the names, but came up empty.

Discouraged, they drove to the bed-and-breakfast. Ruby pulled up beside them and with a shake of her head, exited the vehicle. The team made a somber march to the house and took off their coats, gloves and hats in the foyer.

Donovan waited in the sitting room, phone pressed to his ear. At their entrance, his countenance fell. He placed the call on speaker. "They're back, Veronica. Based on their expressions, I'm guessing they found nothing?"

"Nope." Brandie sighed, dropping onto the closest seat. Her feet throbbed, but she wouldn't complain.

Dylan reached for his phone. "Here're the bomb pictures." Within a few seconds, a chorus of cells rang. "The bomber's using Louter's signature."

Each studied their screens.

"We never released the details of the intricate braid to the public," Dylan explained.

"Are you certain?" Donovan asked.

"Positive," Dylan said. "It was the one significant feature, setting Louter's bombs apart from others we'd seen."

"It's late." Donovan rose. "Get supper, and we'll resume at first light."

"I'll head your way, Veronica," Ruby said.

"Zoe and Nick stopped over with an early dinner and they are both out cold on the couch, and Leah's watching a movie. I hate for you to disturb them."

Ruby glanced expectantly at Dylan. "I have two spare rooms and the couch is a sleeper sofa," he offered. "Stay at my house."

"Wow, you planned in advance for company." Ruby laughed.

Dylan shrugged solemnly. "Something like that."

Did his family visit often? Or was he hoping for a large family of his own?

Ruby headed out with the plan to meet up in the morning.

"I don't mind working through the case a little more," Brandie said.

Dylan shook his head. "It's too late for me to contact anyone at Seattle PD."

Brandie glanced at the clock and winced. "I didn't realize what time it was." She surveyed the room. Star lay curled up on the rug. "How're the dogs doing?"

"They're fine at the kennels," Donovan said.

"Thanks for taking care of them." Brandie gathered her belongings. Star stretched and strolled to her side. "I'm grateful you're with me," she whispered, comforted by the K-9.

She watched as Dylan and Donovan entered their respective rooms. They'd rest and take on the bomber tomorrow.

And Brandie had ideas where to start.

Morning sunlight beamed through the window, casting caramel highlights through Brandie's dark hair. Dylan sat across from her. Both nursed enormous mugs of black coffee. Leah had raked him over the coals first thing, and his ears still burned from the berating. He couldn't blame the kid, but he had no choice. She was safest away from the investigation. Even if it meant suffering her disdain.

"She's going to hate me when this is over," Dylan mumbled.

"She's a teenager," Brandie replied with a grin. "Chances are good Leah's mad at the world most of the time. She just shifted her focus to you for a while."

"Ugh." He attempted to swirl the liquid in his mug without success. "Who made the coffee?"

She peered over her shoulder then whispered, "Donovan. He's kind of proud."

"It's thicker than most of the motor oils I use." Dylan sipped and cringed.

Brandie chuckled. "Did you get much sleep?"

"Nope, but not for lack of trying." He glanced again at his watch. "Think it's too early to call the prison?"

"Can't hurt to try. Veronica wasn't able to reach anyone yesterday. Although on a Sunday that's not unreasonable since the office personnel wasn't working. We need to know if Louter is still incarcerated. That'll tell us where to start."

Dylan dialed the number, and was about to disconnect after the fourth unanswered ring. Finally, a woman snapped, "Prison."

"Good morning, this is Officer Dylan Jeong with the Pacific Northwest K-9 Unit. I'm looking for information regarding an inmate there."

He waited for what seemed like an eternity before the woman asked, "Name?"

"Irving Louter." The words tasted as bitter as the coffee in his cup.

"Just a moment." The receptionist placed him on hold with easy listening music filtering through thick static, then she replied, "We have no inmates named Irving Louter."

Dylan sucked in a breath. "What? How's that possible? He has a life sentence."

Brandie held his gaze, wearing a quizzical expression.

"Says here Louter's deceased. You'll have to talk to the warden for details."

He'd prefer not to go that route, but this was important. "Would you please patch me through?"

Without answering his question, clicks echoed across the line along with the static music. A series of rings preceded a man's response. "Warden's office."

He recognized Jake McDowell's voice. "Hey, Jake, this is Dylan Jeong."

Brandie glanced up for a moment, then resumed typing into her laptop.

"Dylan. It's been a long time."

"Yes, sir." He'd avoided contact with those involved in Louter's case. Now he was asking for favors. Nice.

"You still with Seattle PD?"

"No, I took a position with the Pacific

Northwest K-9 team." Dylan prayed he didn't ask a lot of questions.

"I've heard good things about them."

"It was a great career change." Dylan continued before they went down memory lane. "I'm calling about Louter. He's deceased?"

"Yes." A long sigh. "He and another prisoner brawled last week. Louter got shanked." The warden used the slang referring to a handmade knife made illegally by inmates.

"No kidding."

"Why do you ask?"

"I'm working a case here." Dylan didn't add the unspoken implication that he'd not discuss details. "Did he have a cellmate?"

"Of course," Jake snorted. "This isn't the Ritz."

"I need to visit him."

"*Him* is Alfred Johnson, and he was released a couple of days ago."

"Great." Dylan ran a hand over the back of his neck. "Anything you can give me is appreciated, Jake."

"Let me pull up the visitor log for Louter."

Again, Dylan was placed on hold. He quickly updated Brandie. "Wow."

Jake returned. "Irving didn't have visitors."

"The entire time he's been there?" Not impossible, considering the little he knew of Louter, but it seemed strange.

"No, but I asked to have his personal belongings brought up to my office. I'll call you once I have that."

"Thanks, Jake. I appreciate your help."

They disconnected, and Dylan faced Brandie. "Louter died last week. He's not our bomber."

"That narrows our hunt to a copycat."

Donovan and Ruby entered the dining room, aiming for the coffee station. Both returned to the table, sitting opposite Dylan and Brandie.

Ruby took a sip and grimaced. Dylan and Brandie shared a grin before updating them on Louter.

"We're waiting for the warden to call back with information," Dylan explained.

"It's plausible the cellmate learned of

Louter's signature and opted to pick up where he'd left off," Donovan said.

"Agreed. But why?" Ruby asked.

"A pact they'd made? He was released a couple of days ago, which gives him opportunity to come here and set the bomb," Dylan said. "Louter loved to attack around Christmas and New Year's, though he focused on bigger cities. Why here? Emeryton is a blip on the map."

Brandie turned her laptop—once more grateful she'd not taken it with her in the car when the accident occurred—and revealed her internet-search results of the team and related parade features. "If he targeted you prior to the bombing, the feel-good stories mentioning PNK9 provided the map."

Donovan's cell rang. "It's Veronica." He answered, placing it on speakerphone.

"Didn't we already have this greeting at oh dark thirty when I left this morning?" Ruby teased.

"Yes, Ruby," Veronica chuckled. "For everyone else, good morning."

Dylan's phone chimed and he excused

himself from the table to answer and allow the team to talk.

"After we spoke, I retrieved Louter's stuff myself," Jake said. "You wouldn't dredge up this nightmare if it wasn't a big deal."

Dylan's throat constricted. "You got that right."

"Get this. Irving received letters regularly from an anonymous sender over the course of the past five years. They started almost immediately after his incarceration."

"A groupie or fan?" Dylan slid into a chair near the entry.

"Maybe. They're not handwritten, but the sender always signs 'no impact, no idea.'" Jake paused. "Does that mean anything to you?"

Dylan couldn't breathe. The walls closed in on him, dragging him to his military days. In his mind, the helicopter blades whipped overhead as soldiers rushed to him for rescue. Jake's voice melded into the background.

Brandie approached. "Dylan?" She touched his hand and he jerked away. A fleeting expression of hurt crossed her face as she turned and walked away.

Great. Realizing Jake was speaking, he said, "Sorry, Jake. Say again?"

"Louter had no next of kin. I'll send these to you."

"I'll ask a team member to pick them up today," Dylan offered. "What're the postmarks of the envelopes?"

"Give me a second." Shuffling papers filled in the background. Jake groaned. "Seattle."

"Ugh," Dylan replied. "We'll find him. Thanks again, Jake."

"No problem. I'll have them ready for you."

They disconnected, and Dylan returned to the room where his teammates waited with expectation on their faces. He relayed the information he'd learned from Jake.

"Who was Louter's ex-cellmate again?" Veronica asked.

"Alfred Johnson," Brandie replied.

"What's 'no impact, no idea' mean?" Ruby asked.

"It's a military phrase sometimes used if

a shooter on the range is so far off target that spotters don't see an impact. Loosely translated, it conveys the person speaking doesn't understand an idea or that someone is totally clueless," Dylan replied. "Louter was dishonorably discharged from the army, so he'd be familiar with the term."

"Or whoever was working with him was also military-trained," Donovan said.

"Yes," Dylan replied. "Jake said he'd have the letters ready for us."

Donovan stood. "I'll pick them up. I've got friends at the state lab. Maybe they'll help fingerprint the letters. Then we can track the sender's address and figure out the connection."

"I'm on it," Veronica assured.

"Great." Donovan moved toward the door. "Continue working the clues here." He hurried from the room.

"Whoever Louter's copycat is, they had insider knowledge of the prior cases, or got Louter to share the details," Ruby said.

"Aha," Veronica chimed in. "According to the parole information, the last known address for Alfred Johnson is in Seattle. I'll send the address to Donovan."

"Excellent work!" Dylan lifted his phone. "I'll call Seattle PD and ask them to bring in Alfred for questioning. They can't hold him for long, but as an ex-inmate, he might cooperate to avoid being sent back to prison."

Dylan called his old captain at the PD, again wincing at requesting favors after he'd ghosted his prior coworkers. To his relief, the commander responded without the third degree. One thing he appreciated about shared history was not having to explain himself. Once he mentioned Louter's name, the unspoken urgency fulfilled his reason for calling.

"I'll be in touch," the captain said, then hung up.

Ruby and Brandie glanced up at Dylan.

"Well?" Brandie asked.

"They're going to bring in Johnson for questioning." Dylan offered nothing else.

"You must have some serious connections for them to agree so quickly," Ruby replied.

"Yeah." Dylan didn't elaborate and he

prayed that somehow, he wouldn't have to, because revisiting his past wasn't something he wanted to do.

Not now.

Not ever.

FIVE

Dylan's evasiveness wore on Brandie's nerves, propelling her determination to expose what he was hiding. No leads left them stuck in the same place.

They sat at the dining table, focused on their laptops, quietly going through Louter's original case files. If he'd had an accomplice, as the team agreed was probable, they'd find some communication trail and identify the person. So far, they hadn't accomplished that goal.

They'd received the redacted file version as Dylan was no longer an active officer with Seattle PD. Brandie noticed additional redacted lines with a slight variation in the color, indicating text eliminated after the fact. Was Dylan responsible? If so, why?

She cleared her throat. "We're missing something."

"Nah, we'll find it." Dylan stared at his computer.

"That's hard to do with these documents." She sat taller. "Are you sure this is all you have on Louter?"

"Uh-huh." His phone rang, interrupting the conversation.

Brandie stretched her back, listening intently.

"I know." Dylan met her gaze for the first time since they'd started the research work in the sitting room. "Just add it to the list. No, you can't." He rolled his eyes, shaking his head.

Brandie concluded that Leah was the caller. Poor kid had to be bored off her gourd. Veronica and Leah had moved to Nick's place for a change of scenary earlier that morning, but his internet router had gone down, forcing Veronica and Leah to return to Dylan's home. The unknown danger kept them hypervigilant, moreso since they'd not encountered further attacks. The fact that Dylan's home wasn't listed in his name, remained an interesting morsel Brandie hadn't yet dissected. It had activated her curiosity regarding his secrets. He'd withheld an explanation as to the reason why, and as there wasn't relevancy to the case, no one had pressed.

"Soon. I promise." He pocketed his phone, stood and began pacing around the room. "I have a new appreciation for my sister's struggle in parenting responsibilities."

Brandie chuckled. "Teenagers are easy, said no one ever."

"Preach, sister," Dylan joked, revealing a hint of his normal personality. "It's not Leah's fault. This was supposed to be a fun vacation."

"Well, let's catch Louter's lackey, and get you two back on vacation track." She smiled, spotting Star sprawled on her side. The German shorthaired pointer stretched all four paws in unison and a squeak emitted from her as she yawned.

From the corner of the room, soft music played on the radio in the background. Warmth emanated from the fireplace as the flames crackled. Tasteful lights and a Christmas tree covered in varying ornament sizes and topped with a red bow at the top completed the festive scene. If only they were here celebrating instead of investigating.

The reminder had Brandie refocusing. Time to try a new approach. "I'm stumped. Nothing in the documents offers helpful leads."

"Yeah," Dylan mumbled. "That'll change once Seattle PD tracks down Alfred."

Brandie's cell rang. "Veronica and Ruby." She answered on speakerphone, "Good morning."

"Well, it's morning," Veronica groused.

"Don't mind her, she hasn't had coffee yet," Ruby replied with a chuckle.

"What's the plan?" Brandie asked.

"Since the last carol didn't play out, let's advance to the next on his list," Dylan said.

"I thought you'd say that. I've searched tourist attractions in the area," Veronica replied. "The Holly Peaks Amphitheater stands out."

"Yes." Brandie's enthusiasm increased. "Holly is in several carols."

"Exactly." Dylan spread out the Emeryton visitor's map on the dining table. "Most of the venue is outdoors."

"Making it easy for the bomber to access the property," Brandie concluded. "Good place to start the search."

"A concert is scheduled there tonight," Ruby added.

Brandie jumped to her feet, startling Star, who jerked upright. "Sorry, girl." She grimaced. "I scared Star," she explained.

"Don't mess with our best resource," Donovan chimed in, joining the meeting.

"Aw." Brandie stroked the dog behind the ears.

"Brandie and I will check out the amphitheater," Dylan said.

"Okay, we'll continued digging into the other lyrics," Veronica replied, then disconnected.

Brandie snatched her phone off the table and ascended the stairs to her assigned room. She put on her gloves, coat and hat. When she reached the foyer, Dylan was dressed in his parka and hat with Star leashed. "Ready?"

"Wow, you're fast."

He grinned.

They exited the bed-and-breakfast and strode to Dylan's SUV, which he'd already remote-started. The chilly morning air had Brandie snuggling deeper into her parka. An arch on the windshield from the defroster separated the frosted glass. He unlocked the doors using his key fob and she loaded Star in the back seat, then climbed into the passenger seat.

"Donovan contacted the event manager, Neal O'Brien. He'll meet us there."

"That should speed things up," Brandie said.

The drive was short to the amphitheater and neither spoke during the commute. Dylan parked in the space closest to the building's entrance. Brandie climbed out and secured Star's halter, which indicated the dog was expected to go to work.

A slender man stood at the doors, concern creasing his narrow face.

"Dylan and Brandie?" he asked before they introduced themselves.

"Yes, sir." Dylan extended his hand, which the manager shook.

"Neal O'Brien. Let's get in there." He opened the doors, allowing them entry. "The bands need to set up soon. How long will this take? Do we have to tell them what you're looking for? What will you do if you find anything? I'll have to refund everyone's money." His rambling hindered any opportunity to reply.

When he finally took a breath, Dylan jumped in. "Sir, advise them we're doing a precautionary check. We'll notify you when we're finished."

"I supposed that's acceptable." He nodded emphatically. "Chief Fanelli implied there was nothing to worry about. Correct?"

Brandie hesitated, unwilling to give the man false hope, but she also not wanting to stress him out more than he already was. "Star is the best. She'll be thorough." That didn't answer his questions, but he seemed to accede.

"I sent the musicians and their staff home

and asked them to return in a couple of hours. Thankfully, the cleaning personnel has completed their duties. This delay puts us behind."

"We'll move as quickly as we can without rushing her nose," Dylan assured him.

"Go ahead." He gestured for them to proceed.

Star led the way, and they began the search in the outdoor auditorium seating. The orderly presentation confirmed the personnel's efforts to ensure the grounds were prepared for the upcoming show.

The morning air had warmed slightly, leaving the atmosphere cool, but not miserable. Clear skies overhead promised a beautiful day.

Brandie followed Star, sniffing a path along the rows of seats. O'Brien stood off to the side watching, and Dylan stayed in line with Brandie.

When they'd made their way through the rows without a single alert from Star, they headed for the stage area. Equipment sat in varying stacks, like giant locking blocks scattered on the impressive stage.

Star meticulously worked from left to right, navigating expertly around the gear, her nose power-sniffing the entire way. They searched the front of the stage to the rear, then entered the inner sanctum of the building and stepped into the long hallway. Doors on both sides were closed and labeled as *kitchen, janitor closet* and *offices*. A large sign hung at the end, indicating the restrooms.

Star traveled to a door marked Employees Only. Dylan shifted ahead of Brandie, testing the knob. "Locked."

They turned, searching for the manager, and found him standing near the entrance to the stage, talking on the phone.

Dylan jogged to him while Brandie and Star waited. After a quick discussion, Dylan returned with keys and unlocked the door, holding it open for Star and Brandie. When they crossed the threshold, Star picked up speed, tugging Brandie to the farthest part of the room. They rounded a tall set of shelves jammed full of boxes in various sizes that separated the space.

Star halted, staring at the table before them.

Her passive alert.

"Um, Dylan?" Brandie said.

He left the area he'd started inspecting and joined them. She stopped him with a raised hand. "Star is alerting," she said softly, unwilling to move her gaze.

He shifted to gain a better look.

Brandie never took her eyes off the deconstructed bomb on the worktable, focusing on the braided wires in place.

Dylan's gaze swept across the table and the bomb. His heart drummed hard against his ribs, his pulse booming in his ears. He visually surveyed the device from where he stood, looking for the trip wire. Was the device active? His observation traveled along the exposed wires, seeking the explosives, so he could determine their current state of danger.

"Don't move," he whispered.

Breathe. The unbidden thought reminded him of Michelle's calming manner. He paused, inhaled deeply, then exhaled. Shifting to the side to gain better access, he reassessed the device. A light above the table illuminated the wires protruding from the small metal box. Louter's preferred ignition source was C-4. Dylan saw no evidence of the product. However, the bomb was in the early stages of assembly.

"Well?" Brandie asked.

Relief coursed through Dylan. They'd gotten here in time. "It's him. The same signature braids are evident in the device's makeup, but there are no explosives attached."

"Did we interrupt the bomber?"

"Possibly." Dylan glanced over his shoulder to where O'Brien hovered beside him, mouth agape.

"What's wrong?"

Was he faking concern? Did he know the bomb was here?

"Why aren't you moving?" O'Brien leaned to peer over Dylan's shoulder and his eyes widened. "Oh, my!" His voice rose an octave on each word. "Is that what I think it is?"

"Calm down and lower your voice," Dylan said.

The manager clamped a hand over his

mouth as though containing the rest of his questions.

A great actor? Not wanting to reveal his suspicions, Dylan ignored him. He leaned close to Brandie's ear. The scent of her perfume wafted to him, interrupting his concentration. *Get a grip, Dylan.* He shook off the ill-timed thoughts. "Walk backward very carefully and let's get out of here. Make sure Star doesn't touch a thing."

"Roger that." She gave a slight tug on the leash, notifying Star of her intentions. The dog obediently retreated with her.

They exited the space.

"Come with us. Now." Dylan fully expected the manager to run away or fight him.

Instead, O'Brien turned on his heel and trailed the team to the far side of the hallway. No one spoke until they were a safe distance from the storage room.

The manager poised his hands on his hips, looking the part of an authority figure, but his quivering voice betrayed his emotions. "What's wrong?"

"Who has access to that space?" Dylan demanded.

"All of the employees," he snapped. "Based on the sign secured to the door."

The sarcasm was unwarranted, but Dylan fought to maintain a calm disposition. He suspected that O'Brien may be involved. No doubt, he'd still pushed to have them continue the show tonight. Had he expected them to clear the seating area and leave? If so, he'd been wrong. Now he'd play innocent. Dylan wasn't buying that without more information.

"You know there's a bomb in that room." He watched O'Brien for any signs of deception.

A gasp and the manager's eyes widened again. "No! How? Why?" He shook his head and turned toward the employees-only room.

Dylan placed a hand on his arm, stilling him.

"Are we going to die?" The man's lip quivered.

"No," Brandie replied. "However, we also

don't want to hang around any longer than necessary."

"We need a list of employees authorized to enter the room?" Dylan pressed.

"I—I d-don't know," he stammered. "My secretary handles the personnel files."

"Call her," Dylan replied. He watched the manager, and though the man was clearly distraught, Dylan remained skeptical of his innocent act. "We'll notify the bomb squad. They'll take possession." He gestured toward the room. "Do not let anyone near here. We need to vacate the building until they've cleared it."

"There's no one else inside."

"Good," Dylan said.

O'Brien lifted his phone and swiped at the screen with a vengeance. His voice rose as he barked orders at his secretary, based on the limited conversation Dylan overheard. "Well, find out... We do? When did we start doing that?"

Brandie met Dylan's glance and her lips quirked. They moved out of earshot of the enraged supervisor.

"I'm guessing he's more of a hands-off

kind of guy," Dylan said. "I'm not buying the clueless act either."

"I think you're right," Brandie said. "And he's passing the blame."

"Not for long." Dylan swiped his phone and typed a quick message to the team, notifying them of the find.

Brandie requested the Emeryton police bomb squad to respond.

"We need to vacate the premises," Dylan said loudly enough for O'Brien to hear him.

The man acknowledged Dylan with an annoyed nod and stormed down the hallway with them, phone still pressed to his ear.

"I'll move to the end, just in case he gets any ideas," Dylan whispered.

"Roger that." Brandie and Star led the way.

Dylan waited for the manager to go ahead of him.

Brandie and Star rounded the corner and disappeared from his view. Then he heard her voice. "Dylan?"

He rushed to where Brandie stood beside

the women's restroom. Star remained un-
moving, staring at the ajar door.

The manager stumbled backward. "Is
there another bomb?"

Another bomb.

Two words that raised Dylan's instincts
to panic mode.

The first one was a ruse.

"Go!"

Brandie's wide eyes met his, and she
bolted into a run. "Star, come!"

He gripped O'Brien's arm, dragging the
stammering man through the closest exit
doors.

They rounded the corner of the building
just as an explosion rocked the amphitheater. The force sent Dylan and the manager
airborne and both slammed down on the
hard cement.

Debris rained around them, and Dylan's
ears rang with such intensity that he
squeezed his eyes shut to fight the pressure.

Beside him, O'Brien whimpered and
rolled to his side.

"Are you hurt?" Dylan called.

"No," the man replied, pushing up to a sitting position.

Dylan turned his head, searching for Brandie and Star. His gaze roamed the area, now dusty from the explosion. "Please, Lord," he whispered in prayer.

Finally, something in his peripheral vision drew his attention. Star and Brandie lay prostrate on the ground.

Neither moved.

"No. Please, no." Dylan got to his knees, then stood. He staggered to them.

Had he cost Brandie her life too?

He dropped next to her, inching closer. Brandie stretched her arms upward, releasing the leash.

Star got to her feet, giving herself a thorough shaking.

"You're alive." Dylan lunged forward, embracing Brandie.

"Ouch," she winced.

"I'm sorry." He released her and helped her to stand.

O'Brien stumbled toward them, his pants ripped and his jacket torn.

"Yeah, that was a little too close for

my comfort," Brandie said, surveying the damage.

Dylan reached for his phone. "Mine too."

"I can't believe that happened," the manager gasped, joining them.

If only Dylan could say the same.

But he knew.

This was just beginning.

SIX

"This is so unfair!" Leah bellowed, hands fisted on her hips. "It's Christmas eve!"

The mirror image of her mother, standing in Dylan's living room.

"Leah, I have to work." Dylan's head ached with the banging of a thousand gongs. Worry consumed his mind, and his niece's adolescent temper tantrum was the last thing he wanted distracting him from the case. "I'm sorry, but the team needs me."

"Team. That says everything. If it's a *team*, why are *you* needed? Surely, someone else can fill in for you. Trade shifts. Mom does that all the time at the hospital."

"Your mom is a nurse. My job is different than hers. Most of our team is on vacation out of state."

She rolled her eyes and spun on her heel.

"You don't have to understand it all, just please be patient."

Leah stormed past him and slammed the bedroom door so hard it rattled the pictures in the hallway.

Ridge glanced up from where he reclined on the couch with an expression that seemed to say "not cool."

"Don't look at me that way. This is all new to me too," Dylan replied to the dog.

The Saint Bernard quirked a furry brow and repositioned himself, resting his massive jowls on his outstretched paws. Dylan moved closer and dropped to sit beside the animal. "Lord, we need help," he whispered, gently stroking Ridge's soft fur.

His cell phone chimed and Dylan glanced down. *Unknown*, flashed on the screen and he swiped to read the text message.

How many more will die because of you?

Dylan sucked in a breath, staring at the device. The words pierced him, exposing the guilt and self-reproach he'd carried since Michelle's death.

Too many had died because of his pathetic failure to help and protect them. He knew the exact number, and visions of his days as a helicopter pilot ploughed into him with the force of a sumo wrestler. It had been his job alone to extract teams from behind enemy lines. He'd done it well for so long, until his overconfidence had made him stupid.

And the single time he'd failed had cost an entire team their lives...

Or was the message referencing Michelle and K-9 Pete's deaths in Seattle?

What difference did it make? The body count he felt responsible for was horrific.

No matter that the PD had cleared him, and the military had determined the attack was unavoidable. Both stated he wasn't liable for the lives under his watch.

But they were wrong. He'd failed them all. Dylan Jeong was the catalyst for their deaths.

How many more will die because of you?

And what would happen if Brandie and

the team were added to his unforgiveable death toll?

He couldn't bear the thought.

A knock startled Dylan, and for a second he had to orient himself to his surroundings. He rose and walked to the door in a zombie-like state. Glancing through the peephole, he spotted Brandie outside with Star. Dylan slid the phone into his shirt pocket and opened the door.

"Hey." Her gaze flitted over him. "Are you okay?"

He nodded, trying to find his voice. No. Rather than lie, he replied, "Come in."

Brandie's peaked eyebrow conveyed concern as she entered the house.

Dylan turned and walked to the sofa, where Ridge lay sprawled out. "You gotta move, buddy."

The Saint Bernard yawned and dragged his paws back toward his body, then slid off the couch in an exaggerated slow effort.

Brandie chuckled. "I could've sat somewhere else."

"He's not supposed to get on the furniture, but I didn't have the energy to fight with him too." He gestured at the hallway leading to the bedroom.

Brandie frowned. "Still not going well with Leah?"

"No. She's furious with me. Thing is, I don't even blame her." Dylan groaned.

"She'll be all right. Anger won't kill her."

"Easy for you to say."

Brandie unleashed Star, permitting her to meander the house. "I've been thinking about Louter."

"As if there's anything else to do?" Dylan replied sarcastically. He exhaled. "Sorry. That was uncalled for."

"It's okay." Brandie gave his hand a reassuring squeeze. "Everything we need to know lies with him, and his prior practices."

Except the text message Dylan received did not fall into Louter's normal pattern of behavior. He couldn't share the information with Brandie without explaining what the comment meant. "This bomber has wandered slightly from Louter's design. Maybe he's putting his own take on the bombs?"

"Perhaps, but won't he use Louter's pattern as a starting point before deviating?" Brandie's gaze seemed to search his and Dylan averted his eyes. "Or has he done anything outside of the norm?"

"He created the ruse at the amphitheater, which is normal." The heaviness of his phone hung in his shirt pocket, weighing his guilt with it.

"What aren't you telling me?" Brandie asked.

Her straightforward question left him struggling to process the words. His past and his tainted history was nobody's business. It would not help them with this case. And entrusting Brandie with those secrets wasn't possible. But he had a responsibility to protect her. If he shared the truth of his Seattle days, Brandie would use it in the research on Louter. And she'd know he was a disappointment.

She was stronger than any woman he'd ever known, and he admired her. But if Louter's copycat learned how important she was to Dylan, she'd be in more danger.

Hiding his past was the only way to protect her.

"Have you gotten an update from Veronica and Ruby?" Dylan asked, redirecting the conversation.

Brandie sighed, irritation evident in her tone. "They're working on the Seattle investigation to locate Louter's cellmate."

He groaned. "Let's get Veronica focused on Louter's background—maybe she'll dig up something helpful."

Brandie frowned at him, clearly not pleased with his diversion.

Another knock at the door.

Grateful for the interruption, he stood. "Speaking of." He hurried to open the door. "Perfect timing."

Veronica grinned. "Okay…"

"Brandie and I were just talking about digging deeper into Louter's background for clues to possible next steps or the copycat's identity."

Veronica settled at the dining table with her computer. "I'll get right on it. I also searched *season* and *jolly*, the next lyrics in the lineup of carols you gave us."

"That's not a bad idea," Brandie said. "Let's tackle several words."

He didn't want to discourage the women, but wasting time wasn't an option. "I looked at facilities or events that had those words in the title or description, and I came up blank."

"What if it's a descriptor rather than an actual place?" Veronica asked.

"Oh, that's good!" Brandie said.

"Season...jolly," Dylan mumbled, distracted as he stared at Leah's closed bedroom door. "Give me a minute—I need to talk to her before we go."

Dylan cautiously approached the teen's bedroom and knocked twice. Veronica and Brandie's voices faded as Leah emerged behind the partially opened door.

"What?"

"Easy, kiddo. I know you're mad but let's not dive right into disrespect."

Leah glanced down. "Fine."

"May I come in?"

She pushed the door wider and turned, then flopped down on the bed, making it bounce.

"I'd like to tell you that everything will be done at a certain time. The thing with my job is there aren't really shifts. We work until the case is solved."

"You have a team. Can't you take one day off to be with me?" The quiver in her voice nearly undid him. "Can't Veronica or Ruby or someone else take over?"

"Our resources are limited right now. We're stuck working together." Dylan leaned against the wall, crossing his ankles. "How do I make this easier on you?"

"Take me with you." She glanced up at him, her dark eyes pleading.

"Oh, Leah, I wish that was possible. But it might require you to wear another candy-cane costume." He gave her a sideways grin, but she didn't return the gesture.

"I'd do that." She pushed both hands flat on the bed and sat up straighter. "Please, can I go into town and walk around while you work?"

"Absolutely not." He winced at the harshness of his words. But the girl did not understand the situation. "You have to stay here."

"I'm sick of being in this stupid house."

She jumped to her feet. "I hate you. I hate your stupid ugly house. I want to go home!"

"That's not a possibility and you know it."

"Get out!" She folded her arms over her chest.

"Leah…" Dylan said quietly, trying to calm his niece.

"Get out!"

Furious, he stormed to the living room. Leah slammed the door again behind him.

Veronica and Brandie glanced up at his approach, concern on both their faces.

"Ouch," Brandie said.

"Did you figure anything out?" he snapped, the question coming out more like a bark.

"Santa Claus visits?" Veronica asked. "He's jolly."

"Works for me. Let's go." He moved to the door and grabbed his jacket. "You okay to stay with her again, Veronica?"

"Definitely." She nodded emphatically.

Dylan didn't wait for Brandie to leash Star. He bolted outside.

He needed air to cool down before he said something he'd regret.

* * *

As frustrated as she was with Dylan, Brandie couldn't help but sympathize with the poor guy. His efforts with Leah weren't going well, and not for lack of trying. She didn't have any sage advice for him, not that he'd asked. Rather, he'd spent more time dodging and deflecting her questions.

Brandie considered the parts of his conversation with Leah that she'd eavesdropped on. Specifically, his comment about the team's limited members and being stuck working together. Did he feel that way about her? Would he prefer partnering with someone else? Had Donovan forced him to work with her?

He might not like his options, but she'd prove he hadn't gotten shorted in the partner department. "Let's discuss the knowns," she suggested.

"We've done that already," he grumbled.

"So do it again."

"Knock yourself out. Tell me if you come up with anything."

Taken aback by his attitude and brush-off, Brandie clammed up. Emotions bubbled to the surface, frustrating her, and she recalled strange memories of the woman she'd called *mother* doing the same. She never offered an explanation as to why Brandie couldn't take pictures, or have friends over to the house. She dismissed Brandie's questions and ignored her, exactly as Dylan was doing.

Hurt. Angry and resolute, she thrust back her shoulders and stood taller. She'd earned her position at the PNK9 Unit without his help and she'd solve this case the same way.

Brandie withdrew the Emeryton holiday-events guide. "There's fifteen different Santa visits scheduled in various places in town and the surrounding areas."

"Well, then we'll hit them one at a time," Dylan replied. "I'll see if Veronica and Ruby can trade off shifts watching Leah and take a few."

"Is Donovan still in Seattle?"

"He dropped off the letters at the lab and they promised to get him something as soon as possible. He's on his way back."

"Sounds like a brush off to me."

He frowned at her with the impatience of a parent to a child. "It's the holiday season so they're short staffed just like us. Worse, we are still without a trace of Louter's cellmate."

Brandie bit her cheek.

"They'll take the surrounding towns."

"Okay." She marked off the events. "Let's start on the north side and work our way south. The mall would offer the bomber the most casualties and it's also the largest search area."

"Works for me," Dylan replied.

Though Brandie tried several times to initiate conversation, he disregarded her without comment. Frustrated, she remained quiet until they reached their first destination. The shopping center with a scheduled appearance for Santa.

He parked the SUV, and she slid out, quickly leashing Star. They entered the busy building where last-minute customers milled in and out of stores, taking advantage of the sales and bargains, providing an abundance of potential victims.

Star sniffed a path, catching the attention of passersby. Brandie and Dylan trailed silently behind her.

After an hour of walking around the mall and enduring Dylan's silent company, Brandie's impatience peaked. "What now?"

"Just give it time," he replied. "I'll check in with the others." He called Ruby and Donovan, and based upon the short conversation, Brandie surmised they'd not found anything either.

"Maybe we've got his all wrong," she said.

Dylan scowled. "Well, if you have a better idea, I'm open to suggestions."

"Wow." She halted and glared at him. "What is your problem?"

"Nothing." He sighed. "Let's just keep going. We haven't finished the Santa scheduled appearance list."

The afternoon sun warmed their outdoor walk, but it was getting late, and her stomach growled. Roadside vendors lined the sidewalks of the town's square, preparing for the evening events. A smattering of pedestrians littered the area.

"At least we can check this out before the place fills up for the happenings," she said, once more trying to engage him in conversation.

"Uh-huh."

Brandie rolled her eyes. "Mind if we grab something to munch on?" she asked, then wondered why she'd bothered to extend the kindness.

"Sure," Dylan grumbled.

They made their way along the street to the town square. The aromas of freshly popped popcorn, roasted almonds and other delights drew Brandie like a beacon. Star sniffed the path on the sidewalk. Drawn by the scent of popcorn, Brandie started toward the vendor, but Star halted by the almond cart.

"Dylan," Brandie said. "She's—" Her words were interrupted as gunshots exploded around them.

Brandie dove to the ground, Dylan beside her, shielding her and Star with his body.

They crawled around the back of the vendor's metal cart, seeking shelter.

Screams from the pedestrians filled the air.

"Where is it coming from?" She twisted to try and see behind her, but her view was blocked by the cart.

Dylan glanced up. "The opposite side of the street."

As quickly as it started, the gunfire ceased.

A long series of silent seconds passed without further shots.

"Is it safe?" Brandie asked, glancing up.

"I think so."

The almond vendor was nowhere to be found. Had he been in on it? Star rose and again moved toward the cart, giving a passive alert to the stand.

"She's determined there's something here," Brandie said.

"Clear the area!" Dylan ordered.

People scattered away from them, and Brandie called for the bomb squad. The officer on the line requested she and Dylan wait at police headquarters. "They're probably starting to suspect us," Brandie quipped.

Dylan didn't respond to her. Instead, he updated the team.

She shoved her phone into her pocket, and they returned to where Dylan had parked the SUV. Brandie loaded Star inside and they drove to the PD.

An officer at the front desk, sporting a sling on his right arm, led them to an interrogation room to wait for any updates. He closed the door, leaving them alone.

"Is this part of Louter's pattern?" Brandie asked once they'd dropped onto two chairs. Star curled up at her feet. "You did good, Star," she praised.

"No. He's never shot at the victims before," Dylan said, running his hands through his ebony hair.

"Dylan, a copycat is dangerous enough. A spontaneous copycat is even worse," Brandie said.

He met her eyes, and she hesitated at the sadness that consumed his dark irises. "I know."

"Please talk to me," she said, reaching a

hand to touch his arm. "We're a team. We have to trust each other and work together."

"You're right." Dylan sighed and leaned back in his chair, but he didn't withdraw from her touch. "This isn't easy for me."

Brandie scooted to the edge of her seat, where she perched, listening.

"You're sitting with a coward."

She blinked in confusion.

He continued. "You're familiar with that whole flight-or-fight response? Well, I'm a flight responder to the core. But the problem is, the things I keep running from are chasing me."

"How so?"

"You know I fly helicopters."

"Yeah, you've helped with searh and rescue efforts and I assumed it was a hobby or something you picked up after the military."

Dylan snorted. "Nope. I was on the helo extraction team."

"Wow."

He looked down, revealing his long eyelashes. "My last mission, things went…bad. I didn't get them out in time."

Brandie gasped and put a hand over her mouth. "Oh, Dylan."

"I received an honorable discharge from the military. They said I did nothing wrong, but that doesn't change the bottom line. Men and women lost their lives because of me."

"It wasn't your fault."

He shook his head. "I chose to pursue law enforcement. I wanted to work with dogs, and I joined Seattle PD's K-9 team. My assigned canine, a German shepherd named Pete, was the best. We were partnered with another officer, Michelle King."

At the mention of the woman's name, an unfamiliar sensation cloaked her. Jealousy? No, that was ridiculous.

Before she pondered on the emotion, Dylan continued, oblivious to her contemplations. "Michelle and I were close. I guess that's pretty much what happens with partners, right?" He glanced up.

Brandie's neck warmed. Was he talking about her? "Right," she croaked.

"We worked the Louter case, and when we were closing in on him, we tracked him to an old warehouse. Pete was hot on his trail when we entered. We didn't realize it was a trap until Louter shot and killed Michelle, then detonated an explosion." Dylan averted his gaze. "I lost my partners and my best friends."

"Both K-9 Pete and Michelle?"

"Yes, but not only them. Michelle was engaged to Flynn Morgan, my closest friend. We were in the same military unit. He never forgave me."

Understanding and compassion flooded Brandie. "Is that why you left Seattle PD?"

"I was so tired of loss and violence. I hoped by joining PNK9 I'd rescue the lost and do something good for a change. Donovan recruited me."

"He's aware of your past?"

"Yes. He's the only one."

She'd misjudged him…and everything about him. Brandie reached over and placed her other hand on Dylan's. "I'm sorry you carried all this by yourself." Brandie was well acquainted with bearing pain alone for decades and understood the overwhelming power it had over one's life.

"I'm ashamed of my failures. And I didn't want anyone, especially you, endangered because of me." He focused on her face.

The agony and vulnerability Brandie witnessed there nearly undid her. "I'm sure that's true for any of the team members."

Disappointment shadowed his expression. "Not in the same way." Their gazes held for several long seconds. "I care about you."

Did he mean romantically? Compelled to comfort him, Brandie leaned forward. "I care about you too. And I'm sorry for all you've endured. I'm grateful to be your teammate and, on this case, your partner and friend."

"Not only coworkers or friends." He swallowed, his Adam's apple bobbing.

"What are you saying?" She blinked, processing his words.

"I have feelings for you."

"Oh. I thought you were saying I wasn't capable of being on this investigation," she replied, unsure how to respond to his proclamation. Brandie winced at hearing her admission for the first time. Could she sound any more insecure if she tried?

"What? No!" Dylan leaned back. "Brandie, you're the smartest, kindest, most thoughtful and intelligent woman I've ever known. I see you as a partner, an equal. I just didn't want you to get hurt."

Her cheeks flushed from his sweet words. "I'm embarrassed now."

"Please don't be. I'd never want you to think that I saw you as anything other than the wonderful person you are." He glanced down, fidgeting with a piece of tape stuck on the table. "In fact, it's not the time, or the place, but maybe when this is over...we could..." He didn't finish the sentence and she was relieved.

She'd found him attractive, fun to be around, smart. Basically amazing. Was that why his dismissal of her on the case hurt so much? When he mentioned Michelle, her first response was a twinge of jealousy. What did that mean? Brandie looked down, sorting through the unfamiliar emotions.

He placed a finger under her chin, forcing her to look at him. And in that moment, she melted into his dark eyes, enveloping her with warmth and concern.

They were definitely not just friends.

A knock at the door had them separating and Brandie flopped back against the chair like a fish out of water. *Classy.*

Her heart raced, and she chuckled nervously as one of the bomb investigators entered with an update.

After another shared glance, they directed their attention to the officer.

"Sorry it took so long. Your dog was dead-on accurate," the officer explained. "We found traces of C-4 tucked beneath that almond stand. How she managed to sniff that out on top of all the other smells in the square is nothing short of astounding."

"C-4? Was there a device connected to it?" Dylan asked.

"No, it was just stuck there with duct tape."

"A ruse to get our attention," Brandie mused.

"Looks like it," the officer said. "You all are free to go now."

"Thanks for your help," Dylan replied.

They collected their things and exited

the building. A slight breeze sent frosty air whipping through Brandie's hair.

Dylan remote-started the SUV, and she didn't hesitate to climb inside after loading Star.

"Why had the bomber placed the evidence there to lead us to the stand?" Brandie asked once they were on the road. "Why not just shoot to kill?"

"Because he's toying with us. Reminding us he's got the upper hand." Dylan flicked a glance at the rearview mirror. "And he's figured out we have Star's skills."

"Wow, this guy is twisted."

"Mind if we return to my place? I'd like to check on Leah." He turned off the main road onto the highway.

"Not at all."

As they drove to his house, Brandie concluded whatever it took she would stand by Dylan's side. They would take down the bomber and make sure Louter got no credit if that was the copycat's goal.

Dylan's admission eliminated any animosity she'd held against him. Brandie recognized the devastation of loss and secrets that burned deep.

Most importantly, Dylan's strange behavior and constant comments to have her stay out of the case weren't bred from believing she was incapable. Rather, he'd sought to protect her, fearing he'd lose her the way he had Michelle and K-9 Pete.

That kind of protectiveness was brand-new to Brandie. No one had cared enough to cover and shield her from the world or pain. For whatever it was worth, that permanently endeared Dylan Jeong to her.

And with the epiphany, Brandie realized something else. She had triggers in her emotions that were holding her back.

Lord, help me to let go of the doubt and suspicion that I carry too easily. Forgive me for slapping it on other people unfairly.

SEVEN

Dylan focused on the road, wishing he'd withheld his feelings for Brandie, instead of blurting them out like a lovesick teenager. Three days apart had helped and he'd enjoyed spending Christmas with Leah. There had been no further incidents, but with the remaining holiday events scheduled in Emeryton, Dylan knew the reprieve was termporary.

However, in a strange way, telling her about Seattle brought relief. Her confessions had floored him. How could she believe he thought she was incompetent? That had never once crossed his mind. No wonder it had been so awkward between them.

Although, since his admission, things were strangely uncomfortable, anyway.

As they neared his house, dread filled Dylan. How would Leah receive him?

Veronica had promised she'd talk with the girl, but that didn't mean Leah was finished unleashing her fury on him.

"You're awful quiet," Brandie said.

"In the military, I had plans of action for combat. Guess I'm resorting to that battle strategy with Leah."

Brandie chuckled.

He appreciated the diversion from their relationship conundrum. "Did Veronica mention anything regarding her conversations with Leah?"

"Not really."

Okay. She'd shut down again. Was she angry at him? She'd scarcely spoken more than a few short sentences since they'd left the police department three days prior.

"Are things going to be totally weird between us?" Dylan asked.

"No. It's fine."

Clearly. Memories of his awkward teenage years came bounding back, along with the apprehension of asking out a girl and having her laugh in his face. Why had he said anything? "Look, sorry. Can we forget about what happened at the PD?"

"What?" Brandie twisted to face him in her seat. "No, not at all. I'm glad you said what you did." She didn't elaborate, leaving Dylan baffled.

"Okay."

Awkward silence.

Just let it go.

"I've been thinking about Leah," Brandie said.

Great. He'd confessed his heart, and she wanted to discuss his niece. "Oh, yeah? Got any brilliant words of wisdom?"

"You know my history," she began.

"Some of it," Dylan replied.

"I was abducted when I was three and raised by my kidnappers—I thought they were my parents. It wasn't until after they died that I started questioning my life."

"I can't even imagine all you've been through."

In his peripheral vision, he caught a glimpse of her shrugging.

"The one good thing is that it's given me new insight into others. When you were talking to Leah, it brought back huge memories for me. My 'parents—'" she used her fingers to make air quotes "—wouldn't allow me to do anything. No pictures. No friends and sleepovers, nothing normal. I was always sequestered alone in the house, and I was miserable. I'd never experienced what other girls my age took for granted."

"Leah's an only child, so she expects to get her own way."

"It's not about giving her what she wants when she wants it. Leah feels trapped." Brandie sighed. "Up until now, have her parents ever just dropped her off with you for an extended period of time?"

"No." This was a first. "My sister's *über*-protective, but they're going through a hard season and needed alone time to work through some stuff." Dylan didn't share the rest of the story because it wasn't his to tell. His sister's marriage was facing a relationship storm, but they were willing to fight for their family.

"Surely, Leah has picked up on that tension too, even if she doesn't have all the specifics," Brandie said.

"Maybe." From what his sister, Tanya, had told him, she and her husband were careful not to argue or discuss their marital matters in front of Leah. However, kids were perceptive. "Wow, I never thought about it in that light." Dylan swallowed. "My efforts at protecting the people I care about are causing destruction all over the place."

A soft blush covered Brandie's cheeks, enhancing her beautiful features. "Your intentions are good, but with a teenage girl, you might need to do more than make demands."

Dylan groaned. "You're so right. Any chance you'd sit down with me to talk to her?"

"Absolutely."

He approached his garage and hit the button, then pulled in and shut off the engine. They exited the vehicle and he paused at the door leading to the house. With a fortifying breath, he shoved it open and entered. Veronica jerked upright from her position on the couch. At her quick motion, her laptop nearly fell off her lap. Summer dozed at her feet.

"Relax, soldier," Dylan teased.

"Guess I'm still a little on edge."

Dylan marveled at Veronica's willingness to help with the investigation after her sister's recent terrifying kidnapping and subsequent rescue. "After all you've been through, you should be at home resting with Jasmin."

"Nah, this is helping more than you know." Veronica chuckled and closed the laptop, setting it aside. "I worked all day, trying to dig up intel on Louter and his cellmate."

"Find anything good?" Brandie released Star and dropped onto the recliner.

"Nope." Veronica swung her feet off the couch. "No offense, but I'm wiped. I'm going to head out."

"Where's Leah?" Dylan glanced at the closed door. "Still in hiding?"

Veronica grinned. "She's fine. Said she wanted to take a nap about an hour ago."

"I'd better wake her up and see what she'd like for dinner."

"All right, I'll catch up with you all later," Veronica waved. "C'mon, Summer." A soft click behind him confirmed they'd left.

Dylan walked to the bedroom and rapped gently. "Leah. It's Uncle Dylan. Can we talk?"

Dead silence.

He tried again. "Leah, your pick of restaurants. Brandie and I are starving."

Nothing. He glanced over his shoulder at Brandie. She shrugged and he reached for the knob and turned it, grateful to find it unlocked. He pushed it open, expecting to see Leah. Instead, her bed remained unmade in the empty room. The curtains waved delicately. "She ran off!"

Brandie rushed in and went straight to the window. "Okay, don't panic. Maybe she just took a walk or something."

"Call Veronica, we have to start searching."

"I'll ask her to pick up Taz since he's a trained tracker." Brandie notified Veronica. She clicked off and said, "She'll be here as soon as possible."

Dylan paced the room, scanning for any

clues as to where Leah might've gone. He came up empty.

At last, tires crunched outside, and they rushed to meet Veronica. She jumped from the vehicle, releasing Summer. "Donovan is picking up Taz since he was closer to the kennels than me," Veronica's face crumbled. "I'm so sorry!"

"No time for that," Dylan snapped. "Okay. Let's get Ridge started."

"You're right," she replied, pulling herself together. "Let's start searching."

"Actually, please stay here in case she comes back. Try tracking her phone." Dylan headed for the house.

They began in Leah's bedroom, gathering scent articles for both K-9s.

Veronica entered the home with Summer. "I'll update you with any leads ASAP."

Star had flopped on the couch. Brandie sent their teammate an encouraging smile.

Dylan couldn't share the sentiment. He'd entrustred Leah in Veronica's care, believing she'd protect his niece.

She'd failed.

Dylan contacted Donovan, who offered

to notify the local authorities, advising he'd be there soon. Brandie notified Ruby and learned Zoe and Nick were both not feeling well. She needed to stay with them but promised to do all she could remotely.

Brandie sidled beside Dylan. Together, they utilized the grid pattern, beginning at the house and moving toward the wooded acreage behind his property.

"There's only one road in and out of this place and she doesn't have a vehicle. She couldn't have gone far," Dylan advised. Unless she'd hitchhiked. He prayed that wasn't the case, because the ramifications complicated matters tremendously. "Ridge is focused on the path to the woods."

They walked over a mile into the forest before the dog hesitated, indicating he'd lost the trail.

"How do I tell my sister her only daughter is missing?"

"I'll talk to her for you," Brandie offered.

"No. It has to be me." Dylan lifted his phone and gasped, staring at the screen. "Leah called! How did I miss that?"

They paused under a copse of trees while

he replayed the choppy voice-mail message on speakerphone.

"Uncle Dylan. I'm scared. Woods." Static filled the line. "Lost. Help."

The last two words drove a knife into his heart.

He notified the team. Jasmin had joined Veronica—via video—and together, they'd attempted to triangulate Leah's phone, but to no avail. "Based on the call, she'd had limited reception before she turned off the cell or the battery died," Veronica explained. "Donovan is pulling up now."

"We'll return to get Taz then we'll have to go old-school and rely on the dogs," Dylan said.

"They're the best resource for searching," Brandie agreed.

They rushed back to Dylan's house and quickly leashed Taz to join them, then traveled through the forest. Donovan also prepared to file a missing-person report.

Ridge picked up a trace at the base of a narrower trail, propelling their hope. They followed the K-9s, allowing them to walk the full length of their twenty-foot leashes.

The last hint of daylight faded, compelling them to use their flashlights. The hike grew tougher as they made their way along the rocky path.

Brandie and Dylan's phones both chimed with blizzard warning alerts.

That meant only one thing. They had to find Leah, and fast.

Dylan's phone rang, forcing them to stop. "It's Donovan."

"Return to home base," the chief said.

"We're still looking."

"The predicted inclement weather poses serious danger. We'll continue when the storm passes."

"It might be nothing," Dylan argued. "All due respect, I'm not leaving until I find my niece." He looked at Brandie.

Donovan sighed. "The park ranger has a small cabin—"

"I'm familiar with the place," Dylan interrupted.

"He's on vacation," Donovan replied.

"I have the key code."

"Keep me updated."

"Will do." Dylan disconnected, sharing

312 Holiday Rescue Countdown

the update. "You should go back. Nick will kill me if anything happens to you too."

Brandie shook her head. "Nick would understand your fear. Remember, he lived it personally when I was abducted. He's also a father and knows firsthand what we're dealing with. I'm not leaving you alone out here."

Touched that she'd remain with him, Dylan swallowed hard. "I can't leave without Leah." He hated the quaver in his voice.

"We can't." Understanding flowed from her eyes.

"Donovan suggested holing up at the park ranger's cabin on the other side of the mountain if the storm really comes in. He thought Leah might've gone there too." Except if that was the case, why not use the phone to call Dylan?

"If we get stuck out here in a blizzard, there will be no one to help her or us."

"Just a little longer, please?"

"Okay."

Light flakes peppered the path by the time they reached the cabin nestled beside a *Y* in the road. Several fallen trees to the side marked off the end of the trail. They'd be forced to go to the right or the left. But which way? No lights illuminated the cabin.

"Did I hear you say the park ranger is on vacation?" Brandie asked.

"Yeah. He's gone until after New Year's." Dylan glanced at the structure. "Leah?" He called several more times, his voice echoing his desperation.

Brandie checked the perimeter. "I don't see any sign of her."

"Me either."

Taz tugged on the leash, moving to a clearing opposite of Ridge's position.

Brandie held him back. "Taz, what's going on?" The shepherd didn't relent.

"Did he pick up on her scent?" Dylan asked.

Brandie withdrew Leah's scent article again and the K-9 returned to the same place. "He's stuck on something." She glanced at where Ridge continued sniffing, away from Taz. "This is really unusual— why would they part ways?"

"Which do we follow?"

"Both," Brandie conceded.

"We don't have time for that," Dylan said.

"It'll double our chances of finding Leah."

He quirked a brow, comprehending her meaning. They had to separate. "Okay, but we can't linger."

"Thirty minutes max," Brandie said. "Then meet here."

"No. That's not smart. We should stay together."

"I can take care of myself," Brandie snapped.

He hesitated a second, recalling their earlier discussion. "No more than a half hour. If the storm doesn't last, we'll resume when it passes."

Brandie's feet moved swiftly over the ground as she worked to keep up with Taz's nose. She swept her flashlight beam across the land as twilight descended.

They trekked deeper into the woods, where rock formations added to the landscape and thick tree coverage canopied overhead. He led her to the side of the rocky mountain ledge, where the foliage sprouted between the stones and boulders tucked into the dirt. As they rounded the crag, Brandie paused.

In the distance, a darkened opening surrounded by brush caught her eye. She lifted the flashlight, surveying the area.

A cave! The logical place for the girl to seek shelter until her uncle found her.

"Yes!" Brandie put both hands near her mouth and called, "Leah! Leah!"

She reached for her phone to notify Dylan.

No reception.

Of course.

She couldn't turn back when she was so close.

Brandie resigned herself to the option of finding Leah and reuniting her with Dylan in a wonderful surprise.

Hurrying her steps, she traversed the rough ground through the expanse. The path wasn't established, and she had to navigate the uneven earth to the cave's spot. She drew nearer, realizing she'd have to climb to the edge of the cave.

She released the leash and ordered, "Taz. Stay."

The dog responded with a whine and a bark.

Brandie studied him. The actions weren't his typical indicators, but could be. Dog's sensed emotions. Perhaps he worried for Brandie? "Taz, I'll be right back."

The K-9 sat, tail swishing the fluffy snow.

Brandie shifted to the side, gripping the rock. She placed one foot on the stone and hoisted herself up. Then repeated the process, making the slow climb, until she swung her leg over the small ledge. Using her flashlight, she peered into the mouth of the cave, sweeping the beam to the right.

In her peripheral vision, a shadow passed. The hair on her arms rose.

She turned, just as a slam from behind sent Brandie sprawling forward.

She landed hard, hitting her chin on a rock that was partially buried in the dirt.

A second hit to the back of her head plunged her into darkness.

EIGHT

Large snowflakes carried by wind gusts replaced the light flurries. The darkened sky had taken on a gray quality. All of it urged Dylan toward desperation. Ridge strained at the end of his leash. Dylan released the dog to roam freely near the cabin. "Stay where I can see you," he warned, then returned to pacing the path by the fallen trees, where he and Brandie had agreed to meet.

He checked his watch for the hundredth time.

She was late.

Really late.

He surveyed the area, restrained by the inclement weather that restricted his view. "Come on, Brandie. Where are you?"

Dylan glanced at his phone, though he'd

not heard it ring and noticed the no-service icon. She couldn't call him if she tried.

Ridge strolled near the cabin, his coat covered in a blanket of white.

"We can't wait anymore," Dylan said.

In response, the Saint Bernard trotted to him and nudged his hand.

"Seek Brandie," Dylan ordered, hoping the command would be enough since he didn't have anything of Brandie's to use for a scent article.

Ridge put his nose to the ground, creating a path in the white carpeted landscape. Together, the team headed in the direction Brandie and Taz had gone two hours earlier.

Snowflakes pelted his face, freezing his cheeks and stinging his eyes. "Brandie!" His voice echoed in a mocking repetition. "Taz!"

A mournful baying reverberated in the distance.

Dylan jerked toward the sound. Had he imagined it? Apparently not, since his K-9 also paused, head tilted and ears perked. Was it a coyote or wolf? Another howl.

Maybe Taz? Dylan glanced down at Ridge and prayed he wasn't making a huge mistake. "Ridge, speak."

The Saint Bernard released a low woof, loud and clear.

Nothing.

"Ridge, speak," Dylan repeated.

From somewhere to the east, a responding and familiar bark infused hope, warming Dylan. Taz. He hurried and snapped on Ridge's leash, not wanting to lose the dog in the pursuit of what he hoped was the German shepherd. "Seek."

The Saint Bernard sprinted into the tree line, forcing Dylan to jog in his effort to keep up. "Taz!"

Three consecutive barks. The shepherd's distinct bark alert.

Dylan increased his pace, aiming for the sound. His flashlight beam bounced on the landscape ahead as they deviated from the path. "Brandie? Taz?"

His light landed on a dark figure, swiftly approaching. *Please don't be a wolf.* "Brandie? Taz?"

The object responded by advancing toward him.

Apprehension had Dylan reaching for Ridge's leash and urging him closer. "Ridge, come." The dog obediently shifted to his side.

Had he just alerted a bear to their location? If so, running was the worst thing they could do. The animal would chase them down and attack. He reached for his weapon and watched the figure close the distance between them.

Dylan braced, ready to fire if necessary.

Finally, through the thick brush, the familiar shepherd appeared.

Without Brandie.

"Taz!" Dylan holstered his gun, and the dog rushed to his side. Taz and Ridge offered each other the normal sniff test while Dylan examined the K-9 for any injuries. He was damp from the snow, but otherwise had no wounds. "Where's Brandie?" The dog tilted his head, ears perked in his effort to comprehend Dylan's question. "Brandie!"

Nothing.

Dylan gripped Taz's leash, amazed the lengthy lead hadn't gotten tangled in all the brush and undergrowth. He needed something of Brandie's for the dogs to scent. But it would take too long to return to the SUV.

"Find Brandie," Dylan commanded, hurrying in the direction from where the dog had emerged.

"Brandie! Leah!"

His grip on the flashlight loosened as the cold seeped through his gloves. Ridge and Taz both had thick coats that protected them from the elements, but not for long. If he didn't find Brandie soon, he'd have to take the dogs to the cabin.

Dylan slipped on the icy ground, and he teetered, catching himself before plummeting on his backside. The snow had slowed to a steady tempo, and the wind increased, whipping Dylan's face with frosty blasts.

He continued calling for Leah and Brandie until his voice grew hoarse. His throat burned from the effort and hopelessness settled in his spirit.

An hour later, dejected and freezing cold, Dylan turned around and headed for the park ranger's cabin. "Please, Lord, let Brandie and Leah be there waiting for me." Alternating images of his niece and Brandie contended for his attention.

Guilt, fear and worry collided in his mind, weighing down his steps and his optimism that he'd find them.

This wasn't happening again. He'd messed up and lost two of the most important people in his life. "Please, Lord, I'll do better, give more and attend church every single week. Just protect them and get them home." Though the bargaining was ridiculous and useless, Dylan's desperation overrode his reasoning. "Whatever it takes, God, I'll do it. Please bring Leah and Brandie here safely."

The lingering voice of condemnation that lived in the recesses of his thoughts, along with the painful memories, returned. Dylan wondered why he always became a destructive force in the lives of those he loved. He'd stayed away from relationships, living as a bachelor. Not because he wanted it, but because he feared losing anyone again.

After five years, he assumed it was safe

to open up. To get to know his niece better and to dare to imagine a future with a wife and children.

Brandie's face bounced to the forefront of his mind.

Dylan reached the cabin, frozen and dejected, and removed the dogs' leashes. Both their coats were blanketed with snow. He pulled off the glove from his right hand and attempted to type in the door code. After a couple of tries, the lock released, and Dylan shoved open the door.

The dogs entered ahead of him, and Dylan went in search of towels to dry them off. Both gave themselves a thorough shaking, flinging snow in all directions. He reached for his phone, checking again in the hope there would be service, only to discover his battery was dead. In the rush to leave his house, he hadn't brought his charger. Now what? Should he go home? Should he stay, in case they returned to the cabin? Yes. If he left, Brandie had no way to reach him. He wouldn't abandon her.

He moved in a robotic state, starting a fire in the fireplace, then covering himself with an afghan to warm up. When there was nothing more to do, he slumped to the sofa and put his head in his hands. "Please, God, help us before it's too late."

What was he to do? Should he leave and notify Donovan? As if in response to his unspoken question, the wind whipped with such rage, the lights flickered.

No.

He had to wait out the storm and pray.

A moan, deep and ominous, dragged Brandie awake. Piercing cold pricked at her face, and she groaned, struggling to regain her bearings. The ground beneath her was hard and frigid. The sound returned in a whistling wail.

Brandie stilled, listening.

The wind?

As if confirming her question, an icy breeze filtered to her.

She lifted her hands only to realize her wrists were bound together tightly. Her gloves were gone, and her fingers were so frozen they barely responded to her efforts at wiggling them to revive the blood supply.

A rag suppressed her scream for help and activated her gag reflex.

The darkness prevented her from seeing what her ankles were also tied with.

Her throat was dry, making it hard to swallow against the fabric stuffed into her mouth. Tape secured the gag, tearing at her cheeks.

Fear coursed through her. No amount of blinking cleared her vision. Wherever her current location, she couldn't see an inch in front of her face.

Was she underground? Buried alive? Panic had Brandie pushing to a sitting position. Nausea overwhelmed her senses, and she leaned back, feeling the hard base behind her. She tried to reach overhead, but her effort was hindered by her bound hands. Her fingers didn't touch a ceiling. So not buried alive.

A tiny measure of relief quickly faded. Where was she?

The wind sent another terrorizing moan reverberating in the space. She shivered. Cold seeped into her skin. Brandie forced herself to inhale through her nose to calm down before she surrendered to a panic attack.

She traced the area around her, letting her fingers graze the bumpy floor. Hard and frigid. Stone, maybe?

She continued her examination by touching the wall behind her, the same type of rocky texture. Icy air tainted with the stale scent of dirt and something musty. In the distance, a soft plinking reached her.

Possibly water.

The inky atmosphere closed in on her, overwhelming Brandie in its embrace. Not a hint of light in any direction. The darkness was no doubt intended to keep her disoriented.

Determined to escape and find Leah, Brandie retraced her memory. She'd climbed the rock-strewn edge to the cave.

Then someone hit her. Unable to reach the back of her head, she relied on the dull headache to confirm her recollection of the attack.

The effort brought on a calm disconnect from her current situation, allowing her to adjust to cop mode.

Brandie lifted her hands to her mouth and using her fingernails, tugged at the tape. It took several tries before she ripped off the adhesive. Her cheeks and lips burned from the effort. She spat out the nasty rag, and contemplated screaming.

She paused. Where was Taz?

Should she cry out? Was her attacker nearby?

Her wrists and ankles were bound in front of her, but in the darkness she couldn't tell with what.

A frigid breeze seeped in that seemed to come from every direction.

She shivered again and shifted her position, lifting her chin in defiance. She would not give in to desperation. Brandie pulled her knees to her chest. If she took off her boots, she'd free her legs and walk out of this place. As her fingers grazed the bindings around her ankles, she realized they were too tight, and her plan wouldn't work. However, she instantly recognized the texture of rope.

Hope renewed.

She could cut through it. Brandie leaned

forward, using her fingertips to wriggle the small switchblade from inside her boot. She flipped the blade open and, wielding it like a saw, split the bindings around her feet. If the attacker returned, she had to have the ability to run.

Once the braid snapped free, she placed the knife handle between her knees, blade facing upward, and positioned her wrists over it. Brandie prayed for the skills needed to not slice through her skin. At last, the labor worked, and the rope fell off.

Rejuvenated with the idea of escaping, Brandie braced one hand on the wall and slowly got to her feet, keeping the other hand overhead. Her fingertips grazed the ceiling, confirming her assumption. She was in the cave.

Her phone. Brandie searched each pocket and groaned. He'd taken it and her flashlight.

With her outstretched hand, she felt her way forward. Except which was out? If she went in the wrong direction, she'd walk deeper into the cavern.

Inkiness encroached on both sides with a suffocating obscurity.

Brandie hesitated at a low rumble.

Frozen in place, she considered the possibility that she might not be alone.

A cougar or bear would seek a cave for their home. No, she shook away the thought. An animal would've attacked her when she was unconscious. Additionally, the attacker had brought her inside. He wouldn't do that if an animal resided here.

Something flittered overhead.

Brandie gasped and instinctively ducked.

Images of bats flying had her wanting to scream.

Breathe. Think.

She had to escape the cave. But which way? *Lord, please guide me.*

Air flowed from the outside in. Brandie licked her finger and lifted it in front of her, pivoting slowly until a soft wisp fluttered against her skin.

She turned in the direction of the breeze and again braced her hand along the wall, moving cautiously forward.

Her fingers grazed cold trickles of water

and slippery objects. Thoughts of the people who'd abducted her and pretended to be her parents returned. Until learning otherwise, she had many fond memories with them. One was a family cave-exploration adventure. Why hadn't she paid better attention to the guide? Images of the long, pointed formations hanging from the cavern ceiling had her lifting her hand overhead to ensure she didn't smack into one. What were those called? Stalic? No. Stalactites! She grinned at the term, then snorted. *Go, me, for remembering useless trivia right now.*

Each step was slow and intentional. Her boot bumped into a hard object on the ground. Brandie slowly squatted, touching the thin, pointed formation. Stalagmites protruded from the floor. Impressed she'd recalled the terms, she sighed. *Yep, she was losing it.*

Still, the thoughts kept her from panicking in the dark and gave her something to focus on. Brandie rose again and resumed feeling her way along the walls. She reached a narrow opening. How had the attacker carried her through a small space?

Had she gone in the wrong direction?

Brandie swallowed. Terror, like a cape, fluttered over her shoulders.

No. She had to keep moving. Again, she listened for any sounds that might validate her direction choice.

She contemplated turning around.

Without a light source, she had no way to orient herself.

A soft and damp object grazed her fingers and she jerked away, smacking her elbow into the stone wall behind her. "Ouch," she hissed. Tentatively, she lowered her hand and cautiously examined it.

Moss. Was that a positive or negative thing?

She recalled her parent impersonators, forcing herself not to linger on the few details she'd learned after their deaths. Good had come from that. The investigative pursuit had started her career. She strained to consider the cave-exploration visit, scanning her memory for helpful clues that would get her out of her current predicament. The guide had warned the visitors to stay close and never explore caves alone.

Brandie snorted. Yeah, well, that was inevitable at the moment.

Except she'd spent her adult life isolated by choice. The epiphany stalled her steps.

She'd chosen to disconnect from people socially, trusting no one. Even God. She'd thrust her anger and skeptical attitude on Him. Why had he allowed her kidnapping in the first place? He should've protected her.

Things could've been worse. The couple who had parented her for most of her life had given her the skills to keep fighting. Somehow, though, they'd tried to repress and hide her, but in doing so, they'd ignited the love for research and the purpose of defending herself and others.

And her experience with them at the cave exploration had provided needed steps to free herself.

Had God afforded stepping stones of experiences to equip her for this moment? Is that what sovereignty meant?

Brandie continued walking, her thoughts

drifting to Dylan. She'd not told him that his efforts at protecting her triggered old wounds from her abductors. And she'd shielded herself from pain by not getting close to anyone.

The difference was in the motive for safety. Where she and her parents sought to guard as a source of control, Dylan's concern came from love.

Love.

What did that look like? She pondered the time with Dylan. His worry and concern for Leah wasn't about domination. He loved his niece and had tried his best to keep her safe.

The same way he'd done with Brandie. And she'd refused his efforts with hostility and suspicion. The truth was, she did care for him. Deeply. Was it possible to get past her fear and tell him?

Brandie sighed. She'd seen opposite sides of the same word and that changed everything. Both came down to motives.

She inhaled a fortifying breath, spurred on with the resolve to get out of the cave, find Leah and return to Dylan. Brandie determined she'd confess her feelings to Dylan. She wanted more than friendship too. Warmth radiated up her face at the image of his handsome smile. Hope bloomed within her heart at the possibilities.

After what felt like hours, Brandie halted, tired and frustrated.

The attacker wouldn't have carried her far. And he had to have a way out again. Had he left himself a trail?

A faint illumination by her feet caught her attention. Brandie squatted, fingering the stony floor until she located a small cylindrical object. Plastic, based on the smoothness. Definitely not something authentic to the cave. She crawled and found a second one, still emitting a soft green glow.

Light sticks!

Brandie continued her cautious pursuit forward until a cold breeze fluttered her hair. She hurried on, embracing the frigid air that swarmed her at the mouth of the cavern. Moonlight filtered down, casting an ambient light over the landscape bathed in white.

Whoever had left her here hadn't lingered. Had most likely assumed she'd panic and die in the cave.

A cold-blooded and stupid attacker, because Brandie Weller, aka Lizzie Rossi, was no wimp.

She peered outside, ensuring no one was around, and inched her way to the ledge. Lowering herself down wasn't easy. The slick stones dusted with the newly fallen flakes and her frozen fingers made it tough to hold on. When her feet hit the ground, she wiped her hands on her pants and surveyed her surroundings, locating the path she and Taz had followed.

Her boots crunched on the snow as she walked. At the sight of Taz's partially covered paw prints, she hurried to follow the trail as fast as possible with the limited moonlight.

She located a familiar landmark until a sound stopped her.

Whimpers, like an animal.

Brandie cautiously inched toward the sound. She reached a rocky ledge, where a boulder was precariously close to the edge.

Brandie scanned it, unable to make out any details in the dark. She took a step forward and her boot slipped on the icy ground. With a cry, she slid down the side of the mountain, arms flailing for something to stop her fall.

At last, her fingers grasped a branch. Heaving and hurting, Brandie got a foothold on a rock.

"Hello? Help!" a female voice called. "Is someone there?"

"Leah?"

"Brandie?"

"Leah!" Brandie crawled along the ground. "Where are you?"

"Down here." Leah was lying awkwardly, her leg wedged between two enormous rocks.

Brandie made her way to the girl, spotting her foot twisted sideways. Was it fractured? Not wanting to scare her, Brandie gently touched Leah's leg. She didn't cry out. Not broken, just stuck. "I'll shift your foot and you pull it up."

"Okay," Leah responded. "Be quiet. He might still be here."

Together they freed the teen's boot and scurried from the perilous position.

"Thank you," Leah whispered.

"Can you walk?" Brandie asked, gently examining the girl's leg again.

"Yeah."

They made their ascent up the mountain and onto the ground above.

Brandie led the way to the path.

"Did you see him?" Leah whispered, wide-eyed.

"Who?"

"I don't know. I climbed out the window. Just to take a walk," she quickly added. "When I was around the hill, near Uncle Dylan's, a man put a hood over my head. He dragged me into a vehicle and drove. But I jumped out of the car and ran."

"That was brave."

"Except I didn't know where I was. All the trees and roads looked the same. I made it here and he was following me." Leah shivered and Brandie wrapped her arms around the girl. "I fell and got stuck. The guy yelled for me, then gave up. I couldn't get my foot out from the rocks without sliding down the mountain."

"Did you see his face?"

"No." Leah hobbled a little.

"Lean on me." Brandie shifted closer, putting Leah's arm over her shoulder, bracing her weight.

They moved slowly until the cabin lights came into view.

"We're almost there."

Her stress and fears were alleviated at the familiar barking. The door swung open, and Dylan rushed toward them, embracing both in his arms. "Thank You, Lord. You're safe. I love you."

Brandie stiffened. No. He'd meant the last comment for Leah. Yet, her heart wished he'd said the words for her.

Dylan leaned back, studying them. "What happened to you?"

"I'm f-r-r-e-eezing," Leah said through chattering teeth.

Reminded of her purpose in the case, Brandie shoved away the romantic notions. Now wasn't the time or the place.

"She hurt her foot," Brandie said, avoiding Dylan's eyes for fear she'd blurt her epiphany about them in the cave. "And you need to hear what she has to say." Her gaze surveyed the dark woods behind them, and she shivered. Was the attacker toying with them? Would he return to finish what he'd started?

NINE

Dylan merged onto the highway, tugging down the visor to shield against the last rays of the evening sun. Three days without a lead, and no further incidents had left the team wondering if the bomber had disappeared before he got caught. That was worse than never arresting him. "I still feel guilty leaving Leah at Nick's."

"Leah isn't angry and she loves Zoe. Ruby's busy nursing Nick and Zoe back to full health, so she's grateful for the help. It's a win-win for everyone," Brandie reassured him.

Dylan grimaced. "Yeah, I suppose so." Even in his ill state, Nick had reinforced the order for Dylan to protect Brandie. As though he needed the reminder.

Leah's mild ankle sprain prevented her

from venturing off into the mountains. And the ordeal had fortified the need for extra protection.

"I hate that she got hurt and scared."

"It showed her the danger is real," Brandie said.

"This has to be the worst and longest holiday ever."

"It'll be over soon."

"That's what I'm afraid of," Dylan grumbled.

"We're going to take him down."

If only he had Brandie's confidence.

"He didn't expect you to escape or for Leah to be found," Dylan said, thinking aloud, though they'd already discussed the case a hundred different ways.

"I thought about that too. He lost his leverage with both. Do you think that's why he's not attacked again?"

"Possibly. He isn't finished—he's regrouping," Dylan replied. "His endgame is New Year's Eve."

"Except this bomber isn't sticking with Louter's pattern."

Brandie was right and Dylan couldn't

argue that a short reprieve from attacks complicated things.

"Assuming this bomber's focus is tomorrow," she continued, "we've got one more day to stop him."

As though Dylan was unaware of the date. "I still can't figure out how he located Leah in the woods behind the house."

"He stalked us." Brandie shifted in her seat. "Then struck when the opportunity presented itself."

Dylan didn't reply. Since the kidnapping, Leah's attitude had improved tremendously, with a renewed willingness to cooperate. The shift saddened him because it meant the attacks had beaten her into submission.

They rounded the curve, passing Winterset Camp Site. A spattering of recreational vehicles and a few tents littered the area.

"Those are serious vacationers," Brandie marveled. "I'm not an outdoorsy person to begin with and there's no way I'd sleep outside in this weather."

"Technically, only those in tents fit that description." Some of the campers and RVs he'd seen were nicer than his house. He surveyed the people milling around the area. "I agree with you, though. Not sure I'd be that brave."

They stopped at the intersection, allowing another vehicle to turn.

Dylan glimpsed the driver, then did a double take. With both feet on the brakes, he twisted in his seat and craned his neck to get a better view.

Too late. The blue sedan merged onto highway traffic and headed in the opposite direction.

"Something wrong?" Brandie asked.

"No." Dylan proceeded forward. "I thought I recognized someone." He blinked, assuming he'd imagined it.

Then, he reconsidered his options, whipped the SUV into a U-turn and accelerated, pursuing the sedan.

"Please tell me what's going on?" Brandie gripped the dashboard.

"Flynn Morgan." Dylan searched the area for the vehicle that seemed to have disappeared into thin air. "Where did that blue car go?"

"Are you sure it was him?"

"Nah." Dylan slowed and made a second U-turn, heading in the direction of the bed-and-breakfast.

"Wait. Did you say Flynn? As in your old friend who was engaged to Michelle?"

He nodded. "I'm certain I was wrong," he said, realizing how silly it sounded. "I guess all this bomber investigation has me focused on Flynn and Michelle."

Brandie twisted around in her seat, looking out the rear window. "Should we follow the guy?"

"Forget about it. Nothing more than my mind playing tricks on me."

"Well, it's understandable that you'd think about them."

Except he hadn't allowed himself to do that for a long time. Until the bombing, which had him constantly replaying memories on an endless reel.

Dylan parked in front of the bed-and-breakfast beside the other PNK9 SUVs. They released the dogs and walked up the steps.

Donovan and Veronica waited for them

in the sitting room. Their boss glanced up, wearing a sobering expression.

"What's wrong?" Brandie asked.

"Grab a seat and we'll update you," Donovan replied.

Dylan and Brandie shared a confused and concerned glance as they removed their coats and gloves. Each took one of the chairs opposite their teammates. A platter with cookies sat on the coffee table untouched.

"I received a call from Seattle PD this morning," Donovan said. "They found Alfred Johnson in an alley last night. Dead from an overdose."

"No." Dylan perched on the end of his chair and leaned forward. "That's not possible."

"They also sent this over." Veronica turned her laptop to face them.

Dylan stared in disbelief at the screen—it displayed a crime-scene photo of a wall with the words *No impact, no idea* scrawled in red letters.

"This is the inside of the motel room

where Johnson was staying," Veronica explained.

"That's impossible. He's the copycat," Dylan insisted. "When did he die?"

Donovan shook his head. "Five days ago."

"He can't be the bomber from the Holly Peaks Amphitheater, or the one who kidnapped and attacked me and Leah," Brandie said.

"Right," Donovan replied.

"Now what?" Veronica asked.

Dylan got to his feet, running his hands over his head. Disbelief collided with the recollection of seeing the Flynn lookalike added to his confusion. Their assumptions were all wrong. "We have to start at the beginning."

"How so?" Donovan asked.

"We go back to the carols. The bomber will attack again within twenty-four hours. It will be the worst explosion of them all." Dylan exhaled. "He'll ensure a lot of innocent casualties."

"Then let's get to work," Brandie said, clearing a space in front of her.

Dylan moved to his bag, withdrawing his

copy of the songs. The other members did the same. He dropped onto his chair. "Look at the next carols. Since he didn't attack in the normal order, we have to consider all four." He flattened the creased and wrinkled paper on his leg.

After several long minutes, Veronica leaned back against the sofa where she sat. "Ugh—*yuletide, carol, harp* and *chorus* all stand out."

"That's too many options," Brandie replied.

"Not necessarily." Dylan pointed to the events list on the coffee table. "In what context would you hear those words together?"

Brandie snorted. "Just about every Christmas song listed."

"Songs!" Veronica blurted. "What about carolers?"

"Yes." Dylan nodded. "They'd sing all the lyrics."

"Aren't most finished with that by now?" Brandie asked.

"Emeryton boasts about their endless two weeks of holiday joy. It goes right up to New Years Day," Donovan said and got to his feet, leaning over the events guide. "There are several caroling groups. One is scheduled to visit the elderly assisted-living facility. The other is a combination of local churches. They'll all meet downtown in—" he paused, glancing at his watch "—twenty minutes."

"Let's go," Veronica said, closing her laptop.

Dylan pulled on his jacket. "Brandie and I will join the church group."

"Great. Veronica and I will blend in with the assisted-living carolers." Donovan tugged on his parka. "Keep me updated."

"Roger that," Brandie replied, leashing Star.

Veronica and Donovan left, waving as Brandie, Dylan and Star walked to his SUV.

Brandie moved to the back passenger door to help the dog inside, but the German shorthaired pointer halted, staring at the underside of the SUV. Her passive alert.

Dylan and Brandie hesitated, the realization hitting them.

In what felt like too-slow, and simultaneously fast-motion, Brandie hoisted Star into her arms, and they bolted for the safety of the bed-and-breakfast foyer.

Dylan struggled to get the key in the door. Adrenaline roiled through his body. At last, the lock released and they dove inside, landing on the wood floor with a thud.

The subsequent blast shook the building's foundation, consuming the SUV into flames.

Brandie focused on her laptop. After an unsuccessful search with the carolers, she and Dylan had holed up in the late hours at a library meeting room. "This bomber is audacious. He shows up at the bed-and-breakfast while we're there working, no less, and places a bomb on your SUV? He's stalking us. Toying with us, like you said."

"He's taking this to a whole new level. He knew which vehicle we drove," Dylan replied. "He could've blown up the entire building."

"I'm baffled at how fast he works, setting it up while we were inside the B&B," Brandie shook her head. "He wanted to ensure you were the victim."

"It has a more personal touch to use my SUV," he mumbled sarcastically. "It's late and we've gone through everything forward and backward. You should get some rest and take the dogs with you."

"Good try, but no." She offered him a reassuring smile. "Besides, the last time I checked on them, Ridge was snoring up a storm with Star crashed out beside him in the reading room."

"Well, in that case, a few more minutes of research won't hurt," Dylan replied.

"My sentiments exactly." Brandie focused on her screen, scrolling through the list of parades throughout Washington for the past seven years. Her gaze landed on a feel-good story featuring a video of Flynn Morgan and Michelle King in Emeryton. She leaned closer, examining the image of Michelle smiling brightly, as she showed off her new engagement ring.

In her peripheral vision, Dylan paced beside her. Brandie inserted her ear pods and played the video.

The interviewer introduced Flynn and Michelle, asking them to share their story.

Flynn said, "You never know how things will come together. I shot romance arrows at Michelle for a year. No impact. No idea."

"What's that mean?" the reporter asked.

"It's a phrase used if a shooter on the range is so far off target that spotters don't see an impact," Flynn explained. "I thought my gestures were obvious."

"And I had no idea," Michelle giggled.

"Um, Dylan," Brandie said.

"Hmm?" He meandered to her side, and she spun the laptop to face him, removing her ear pods so he could listen. She replayed the video.

"It's a coincidence." Dylan shook his head slowly, but his drawn expression spoke volumes.

"Flynn knew the details of Louter's case. Michelle probably talked to him and shared things not available to the media. Cops talk cases with their significant others."

"He wouldn't..." Dylan didn't finish the sentence.

"She was the love of his life and blamed you enough to disintegrate your friendship." Brandie got to her feet. "He used the same phrase."

"It's common in the military."

"Except it meant the most to me."

Brandie spun on her heel at the unfamiliar voice. Flynn Morgan stood in the doorway, pointing a gun at them. "Put your weapons on the table and slide them to me. Flinch or try anything heroic, and I'll detonate this place and Nick Rossi's house."

Brandie's eyes widened. "What?"

"Do what I say." He removed a backpack with his non-gun-wielding hand.

Without hesitation, Brandie and Dylan complied with Flynn's demands. He snagged their weapons and dropped them into the backpack.

"Get closer together," he ordered.

Dylan took his place beside Brandie. "Flynn, why?"

"Why?" Flynn snarled. "Are you really going to ask me that?"

"Louter is dead," Dylan reasoned.

"Yep, he is. That was the simplest revenge to take," Flynn replied. "You'd be amazed how easy it is to buy murder in prison."

Brandie gaped at him. "Why now?"

"I asked myself that same question," Flynn said. "But then I saw him." He gestured the weapon in Dylan's direction. "I spent too much time hating you. Lost touch with your whereabouts until your team went viral with all your success stories."

"I don't understand," Dylan replied.

"You took everything from me. You should've died instead of Michelle."

"I agree," Dylan said flatly.

"Louter killed Michelle," Brandie argued, defensiveness building for Dylan.

Flynn sneered. "Because your boyfriend is a failure at all he touches."

Dylan stood taller, sorrow etched in his expression. "We're not dating."

"Save it. I've known you a long time. You're in love with her." Flynn swept the gun from Dylan to Brandie. "But I'll make sure you don't get the happiness with her that you stole from me."

Brandie couldn't take her eyes off Flynn. Dylan in love with her? No way.

Though she'd not told Dylan, her heart testified in agreement.

She loved him.

"Then kill me and let her go," Dylan replied coolly.

Brandie whipped her head around to look at him.

She saw resignation and defeat in Dylan. He'd given up.

After all he'd endured, did he believe himself unworthy to live? Or was he giving his life for hers?

Regret consumed Brandie. She should've confessed her feelings for him. Why hadn't she shared her testimony of God turning the pain and suffering she'd encountered for good?

She'd developed a drive that motitvated her to contribute to the PNK9 team. She'd fought to help others. Though she might never reconcile why God allowed bad stuff to happen, He'd been faithful to use it to help others.

"Dylan," she said.

"Shut up!" Flynn snapped.

They would die tonight, and Dylan would never know that she'd fallen in love with him.

TEN

"Of all the places, you chose Emeryton to mock me?" Flynn snarled.

"No." Dylan blinked, confused. "I wasn't aware this is where you proposed to Michelle until just now when Brandie found the news story."

Flynn cursed. "Right. As if I'd believe that." He paced in front of them. "I even left you alone with your pathetic single, broken existence. You forgot Michelle and me. Moved on without a care. But it's your fault she died."

Dylan bowed his head, unable to deny the accusations. "I think about Michelle every day."

"Don't you dare say her name!" Flynn bellowed.

"I deserve to die, but Brandie's done nothing wrong."

"You don't get it." Flynn jerked to look at Brandie, eyes wild, crazed. "You'll suffer. You came here as a personal affront to me. Showing off your new job and mocking my memories of Michelle with your stupid motorcycle-riding dog. You cheapened everything I care about."

"Is that when you plotted your revenge with Louter?" Brandie asked. "Wrote letters to him?"

They'd not yet received the lab's confirmation of fingerprints on the letters from Louter, and Dylan recognized Brandie's attempt to corner Flynn into confessing.

Flynn shrugged. "Louter and Johnson got off easy. Neither paid enough for their crimes. But you will, Dylan. You're gonna pay."

"Why kill Johnson?" Dylan probed, stalling.

"He used the money I gave him for information to buy drugs. That's totally on him." Flynn gestured to Brandie. "When she dies, you'll grieve as though your entire soul is ripped from your chest. Then you'll understand the pain of losing someone you love."

Dylan swallowed hard. Yes, Flynn was right. He loved Brandie. But if Flynn thought that, he'd kill her. "You've got it all wrong."

"Stop lying! Anyone watching could see your feelings." Flynn guffawed. "Oh. That's it! You haven't told her yet."

Dylan glanced down, neck warm with embarrassment.

Flynn's cackle made goose bumps rise on Dylan's skin.

"That's priceless."

"Please, Flynn. Consider what you're doing," Dylan reasoned. "You're throwing away your life and tainting Michelle's memory. Is this what she'd want?"

"What's it matter?" Flynn cried. "She's gone!"

"But you're still here. How does killing me and Dylan honor your fiancée?" Brandie asked.

"It shows I'm willing to die for her."

"So was I," Dylan replied softly. "I went

in first with K-9 Pete. I told Michelle to stay behind and call for backup."

"Don't blame her."

"I'm not," Dylan argued. "She was a heroine, brave and stubborn. Michelle fought until the very end. I'd have given my life for hers, but that's not how things went down that day. Louter shot her with a scoped rifle. He didn't wait for the bomb. The explosion happened afterward, killing Pete."

"But you survived!" Flynn's jaw hardened. "Just like your cowardly behavior in Iraq."

"I'd give anything to save those warriors. I can't explain why bad things happen." Dylan's throat tightened. "I didn't deserve to live, but I've tried to make amends by helping others." At his confession, Dylan realized he'd ran from the past while running right into the same career. Law enforcement was his calling, drive and mission. He wouldn't apologize for that.

"Flynn, where are our dogs?" Brandie glanced at the door standing ajar.

"Unlike Dylan, I don't harm the innocent."

Dylan's phone vibrated inside his pocket. He coughed, hoping to conceal the sound. "Let her go. This is between you and me. Brandie had nothing to do with Louter. We're not involved romantically." It killed him to say those words, but it was true. He'd told Brandie how he felt, and she'd not reciprocated. He'd not give Flynn ammunition to hurt her.

"He's right. We're just coworkers," Brandie replied.

"Nope. She's as much a part of this as you are." Flynn aimed the gun at her.

"Why not kill me then?" Brandie asked. "What's the point of this tirade? You're not willing to listen to the truth."

The door behind Flynn swung open.

In a blur of white-and-brown fur, Ridge bounded into the room and tackled Flynn, flattening the man to the floor. The gun flew from his hand.

Brandie dove and swept the pistol from Flynn's reach.

"Get him off of me," Flynn grunted as Ridge stood proudly on his back.

Donovan entered, weapon drawn at Flynn.

"Flynn Morgan, you're under arrest." He spouted a litany of charges.

Dylan's focus was on Brandie. "Are you okay?"

"Yes."

Muffled sirens wailed outside, while red and blue lights strobed the room. Veronica entered, followed by several officers from the Emeryton Police Department.

Donovan stood with Flynn handcuffed while he spewed curses and threats.

"That's enough!" Dylan met his ex-friend eye-to-eye. "Where's the last bomb?"

Flynn's lips flattened into an eerie smile. "I'm not saying."

The urge to punch the smug look off his face had Dylan fisting his hands.

Leah entered the room and Flynn blanched. "I recognized his voice when we were outside," she explained. "I'll testify to him kidnapping me."

"What's it matter?" Flynn's jaw hardened. "I have nothing left to live for."

"Because it's the right thing to do," Dylan said. "This isn't you."

"How would you know? When was the last time you even spoke to me?"

Dylan's heart wrenched. "I ran from Seattle, from the pain and memories."

"You abandoned me when I needed your friendship most."

"I won't excuse my behavior." Dylan shook his head. "I'm sorry. But let's make this right. Let's stop the hate and revenge."

"Flynn, stop this. You're disgracing Michelle and all she stood for," Brandie whispered. She gestured at the computer with the picture of him and Michelle still displayed.

"She was my everything." Flynn hung his head. "The final bomb is set to go off at the town-square clock."

"Thank you." Donovan led him from the room.

"How did you know we were here?" Brandie asked Veronica.

"Donovan tried calling and when you didn't answer, Leah and I came to tell you Willow is in labor," Veronica said. "Nick and Zoe are on the mend so they're headed to the hospital with Ruby."

"I'm lost. Back up." Brandie grinned.

"When we arrived, it was obvious something was wrong," Veronica said. "The dogs were locked in the reading room and the door was blocked to ensure they didn't escape. We called for backup and then Leah heard Flynn talking, we braced for the takedown."

"Great work, kiddo." Dylan pulled his niece into a hug. "Flynn knew it was over when he saw your face."

"Thanks, Uncle Dylan." Leah beamed at his compliment.

He held her tight. "If you hadn't come when you did…"

"But they did," Brandie said, squeezing his shoulder.

Veronica sat on the edge of the table. "I never expected Ridge to tackle Flynn."

"Me either. We might need to work on apprehension techniques." Dylan laughed. "You're the best." He kneeled beside the Saint Bernard, who panted happily.

Brandie stroked Star's head. "I'm glad he didn't injure them."

"I'm grateful you weren't hurt." Dylan rose, pulling Brandie into a hug. "I couldn't bear it if anything happened to you."

"Um, Leah, let's go check in with Donovan," Veronica said, ushering the teen from the room.

"You were saying?" Brandie said.

"I'm in love with you." He grinned so wide he thought his face would split in half.

"Oh," Brandie gasped.

Had he made a mistake telling her? Would she reject him?

"I wanted to tell you after I escaped the cave, but it didn't seem like the right time," Brandie began. "Then when I was sure Flynn would kill me, I regretted it. I've lived my whole life cautiously."

"What're you saying?" Confused, Dylan held his breath.

"I'm falling for you too." Brandie looked up at him.

Dylan lowered his lips to hers and all of the things he'd hoped for and dreamed about spurred to reality in one kiss, reminding Dylan he never wanted to be without Brandie.

* * *

Brandie and Dylan scurried into the hospital entrance, meeting Nick in the lobby at eight o'clock New Year's Eve morning. In a single stride, he closed the distance and embraced her. "Thank God, you're okay. I couldn't lose you again!"

She chuckled. "I love you too, big brother."

"Willow is in room 3303."

Dylan paused. "What about the bomb?"

"Donovan said it was defused."

"Yes!" Brandie fist-bumped Dylan.

"See you guys upstairs. I have to run out and grab Zoe's stuffed animal." Nick placed a hand on Dylan's shoulder. "Take care of my baby sister."

Brandie's ears warmed. "You did not just say that."

Nick shrugged. "Get used to it."

She laughed, enjoying this new kind of protectiveness.

They walked to the elevators and entered. As the doors closed, Dylan said, "I'm sorry for everything. You never should've been Flynn's target. I'm not making excuses for him, but I understand why he hates me."

"He can choose to let God redeem his hurt and turn the bad into something good."

"You believe that?"

"Yes, but it's new to me. I've had my own anger issues with God over my childhood abduction, but that time in the cave, and this most recent incident with Flynn, have shown me God's plan is bigger than we imagine and pain is inescapable."

"Flynn wallowed in anger until hatred consumed him." Dylan paused. "I don't want to hang on to my past guilt and shame."

"Good. We have a great future ahead of us, I'd hate to waste time on that junk." Brandie kissed his cheek.

He reached for her hand, and they entered Willow's room. The new mother cradled her baby. Ruby, Zoe, Leah and Donovan were all standing near her, grinning like Cheshire cats. Veronica and Jasmin were also present.

"You look beautiful." Brandie rushed to hug Jasmin and Veronica. "It's great to see the two of you together."

Dylan slung an arm over Leah's shoulders. "You're the bravest teen I know."

"This is the most adventurous holiday ever," she chuckled. "Better than sightseeing and shopping."

The group laughed.

Willow beamed. "Meet our newest team member, Jamie. She's named after my dad."

Brandie's throat thickened with emotion as she approached her friend. Willow had lost her entire family when she was younger, so the name was extra special.

Nick returned and joined them.

"She's beautiful," Brandie whispered.

"Want to hold her?"

"Please?"

Willow passed Jamie to Brandie and Dylan moved beside her.

"It's about time you two got together," Veronica said.

Brandie grinned at the joyful expressions on the group's face. They were more than the PNK9 unit. They were a family. "Hello, Jamie. Welcome to our family."

"Hear! Hear!" Donovan said.

The rest of the team chimed in with collective *amens.*

Dylan whispered, "Happy New Year, Brandie."

"It's the happiest New Year ever."

* * * * *

Dear Reader,

I had the most fun with this story, and I hope you enjoyed it too. Dylan and Brandie both battle with painful past experiences, but they find that God can use anything and somehow turn it for good.

I hope their story encourages you when you're facing a storm in life too.

I love hearing from readers! Please visit my website and join my newsletter at www.shareestover.com for the most current information on my books.

Blessings,
Sharee